PRAISE FO
LOOK CLOSE

"Stewart Lewis weaves an eerie mystery that will haunt and inspire readers long after the final page is finished. A tribute to the bond between father and daughter and a reminder to appreciate the present. It's all any of us are guaranteed."

—Laurie Boyle Crompton,
author of *Love and Vandalism*

"An immersive novel that pulls the reader under and then pushes them to the surface. A compelling story about grief and light, treading water and finding our strides in a turbulent, sometimes mysterious world."

—Emily Franklin, author of
Last Night at the Circle Cinema

"While we often feel powerless, Tegan's story reminds us that even small, seemingly insignificant interactions can have a lasting impact and that life is precious."

—Meg Eden, author of
Post High School Reality Quest

LOOK CLOSER

ALSO BY STEWART LEWIS

Stealing Candy

LOOK CLOSER

STEWART LEWIS

Published by Sourcebooks Fire, an imprint of Sourcebooks, Inc.
P.O. Box 4410, Naperville, Illinois 60567-4410
(630) 961-3900
Fax: (630) 961-2168
sourcebooks.com

Library of Congress Cataloging-in-Publication Data

Names: Lewis, Stewart, author.
Title: Look closer / Stewart Lewis.
Description: Naperville, Illinois : Sourcebooks Fire, [2019] | Summary: After strange messages start appearing, Tegan has the chance to save others' lives--and possibly her own.
Identifiers: LCCN 2018033685 | (pbk. : alk. paper)
Subjects: | CYAC: Grief--Fiction. | Death--Fiction.
Classification: LCC PZ7.L5881 Lo 2019 | DDC [Fic]--dc23
LC record available at https://lccn.loc.gov/2018033685

Printed and bound in the United States of America.
VP 10 9 8 7 6 5 4 3 2 1

for my siblings:

reed, mace, and curt

When one of us gets lost and is not here,
he must be inside us and there is no place
like that anywhere in the world.

—*Rumi*

LOOK CLOSER

1.

i am with you

Even the window is crying. Through the rain-streaked glass, the tree is a muted blur, silhouetted against a greenish-gray sky. Each drop runs down the pane with slight hesitation before free fall, like tears. I can't decide if it's beautiful or an omen. Maybe somewhere in between.

I exist in the world and complete tasks, but lately it feels like I'm just going through the motions. Basically, I'm numb. Here, but not here, as I sit in my kitchen, methodically eating stale Cheerios out of the box.

It's too hot for June. That's all everyone talks about. Weather, weather, weather. I've caught up on all my podcasts and have pretty much Netflixed everything, therefore am bored enough that I'm counting each Cheerio I put in my mouth. I just ate number twenty-three. I'm not even hungry.

My best friend, Jenna, is in California, and I'm stuck in the sticky swamp that is Washington, DC, for the summer. I know I said everyone talks about the weather, and here I go talking about it, but it *is* pretty extreme. It gets so humid here that it physically slows your body down, like walking through a thick cloud of moisture. You shower, and then you have to shower again five minutes later. I don't like to sweat. That's one reason I like swimming—it hides the sweat. I used to compete, but haven't timed myself since I quit the team last year. I still swim at the community pool on the edge of Georgetown, but not competitively.

As a kid, while my friends splashed each other and played Marco Polo, I'd be in the deep end of my neighbor's pool, submerged, eyes wide open in a perfect silence, tiny bubbles leaking out of my nostrils, my limbs moving in slow motion, speaking some kind of language I would never say aboveground. I love my body underwater. Outside of the pool, the world feels confusing and chaotic, always on the verge of spinning out of control.

It's been 402 days since my father died, each one marked by a column of penciled *X*s on my bedroom wall. Counting won't bring him back, but measuring his absence is a way to check in, to let him know I'm still here, that I always will be. Not a day goes by that I don't think about him—the way his smile changed his whole face, the mismatched socks he wore, the dried toothpaste on the corners of his mouth that I wouldn't tell him about because it made him more real.

I'm supposed to say that he died in combat, but he was actually flying a helicopter that was blown to pieces in Syria. As a kid, I listened a lot, even when people didn't think I was. I knew he never wanted to be in the military. My grandfather basically forced him to, and flying rescue helicopters was Dad's way of saying: *Not only will I do this, but I'll do one of the most elite jobs just to show you.* My father was humble, but also very proud. When he came into my seventh-grade class after his first deployment, wearing his shiny medals, I was a celebrity for like, a week. A boy they called Crooked Carl (due to his nose, which I actually liked) even asked me to go to a movie with him. After it was over, his mother was late to pick us up, so we walked over to the train tracks behind the Cineplex. He kissed me while a train was coming. It was thrilling, but we peaked too soon. He lost interest after that. He has a boyfriend now. I joked to Jenna that I turn boys gay, and she laughed, but said, "That's kind of true." I always wanted to have a legit boyfriend, but it hasn't happened yet.

My mother walks into the kitchen and starts gathering the ingredients for her daily smoothie. It's a kind of muscle-memory dance, watching her arms arc and twist to get what she needs out of the cabinet and the fridge. She turns on the blender, which is so loud it hurts my ears. Her smoothie has the consistency and color of mud. She started drinking them after meeting Larry, who I don't really think of as a stepfather. He's more like a guy who wears a gold chain, talks about his money, laughs at his own jokes, and wears too much cologne.

Three months after my father died, when my mother announced she was marrying Larry, I freaked. I started hyperventilating and hurled the glass of water I was holding across the kitchen. It smashed into a hundred shards. Then I bolted up to my room, slamming the door. I didn't come out for days.

Now, my mother takes a sip of her mud smoothie and says, "Mmmm," then gives me the familiar, slightly pained look that makes her way less pretty than she is. "Honey, you can't sit around here all summer without doing anything. You can get cracking on your college applications. And have you thought about getting a job, or volunteering?"

Her eyes bulge, waiting for me to respond.

"I'm still trying to get over the fact that my father is dead, unlike you, who decided to get married six months later."

"Seven. And Tegan, you've punished me enough for this. It's getting old."

She's kind of right. I didn't talk to her for months. And I definitely didn't go to the wedding. It's only been okay between us lately because she threatened not to let me visit Jenna in California next month unless I behave like a "civilized human being." Whatever that means.

Larry comes in wearing his multicolored paisley robe, his smile somewhere between a game-show host and a serial killer.

"Hi-de-ho," he says.

Barf.

There's a Honey Nut Bee pyramid word game on the back of the Cheerios box, and normally I wouldn't give it another glance, except I notice that some of the letters are underlined in pen.

S U J

U T C M S

L H A B T R T

S O A V R D H Y D

D D H U W A R E G T Q

E F T Y H F E W F Y G E P L W

It takes me a few moments of staring to determine the underlined letters spell a name: *Brady Hart.*

"Did you do this?" I ask Larry, who's pouring himself coffee.

"Negatory." He's consumed by his day trading on his phone.

"Me neither," my mom says. "Why, what is it?"

"A name. Someone's name." Weird. Who is Brady Hart? Is it some sort of coincidence?

I put the box down and go back to my room, where I try on some of my mother's old sunglasses she gave me to get on my good side. The cat-eye lenses are too small for my face, but I look okay. My hair is wavy like my father's, and I have my mother's heart-shaped mouth. I choose the black, oversized knockoff Chanel ones and pack my bag with my phone, keys, and water bottle.

I take the Metro downtown. On the platform, everyone is practically hunched over from the heat, sweaty and miserable, including myself. The rain has stopped, but the humidity hangs thick in the air. When the train comes, we pack in and get even sweatier. There's a woman who's eating tuna fish, and it almost makes me retch.

I get off at Gallery Place and am the first one out of the train and on the escalator. At the top, I run across the street and up the stairs to the giant white door of my favorite museum. The air conditioning greets me, covering my sweaty skin with a cold rush of frigid air. I close my eyes in pleasure. This is my place. There are other people here, but I might as well be alone. I walk slowly, in a kind of trance. It is quiet and lovely, and the people around me aren't talking about the weather.

There's a whole room dedicated to a pile of cotton, like a single puffy cloud in its center. Because of all the negative space, it makes it really seem like art. In another room, there are portraits of people with so much pain in their faces that it somehow diminishes mine. There are also flowers and apples and naked, fat women lounging on couches. There are fields with wild geese and boys with shiny, golden swords. Women in bright yellow dresses who have so many stories in their eyes. Ships being enveloped by massive waves, sailors stricken with fear. It is only the rooms with art depicting battle that I avoid. Still, there are reminders of what I have lost everywhere: fathers and daughters holding hands, people in uniform, a kid playing with a toy helicopter, a Black girl in a camouflage skirt.

This is why I stayed in my room for so long, listening to podcasts and watching Netflix. Although the reminders were there, too. A story line about a soldier, some kids playing "war." A journalist talking about being in Syria and losing her husband in a bombing, how she was left holding his hand, which was detached from his body. This is the kind of horrible stuff that happens. But you always think it happens to other people. Except, it happened to me. And I know it's strange, but it feels like he gave me up for his country. Yes, it was a noble way to die, but for a while I hated him for leaving me behind. Now, I am left with only a deep sense of longing. I'd trade anything to see him smile one last time. Anything.

I sit down on one of my favorite benches near the van Goghs and take a bunch of deep breaths. I listen to the tapping of the shoes on the shiny floor, the rattle of the air conditioner vent, the soft whispers from the people going in every direction. Sometimes simply being in the world is the right distraction. I sit for an hour or so and then head back outside into the wall of heat. Downtown DC is milling with young interns and bankers who are in their own worlds, staring at screens while rushing to meetings. I am usually in my own world, too, but for some reason I look up at the people around me. A woman with red hair in a flowy white dress walks toward me. I think she's going to say something to me, but she simply smiles. It's a real smile not only on her lips but in her eyes. It catches me off guard, and I stop in the middle of the sidewalk.

Then I hear a kid say, “Hi.” I look to where the voice is coming from. Across the street, a young boy stands and waves at me with one hand, his other holding the hem of his mother’s skirt. He smiles, too. I start walking again, and a man bumps into me, says, “So sorry,” in a thick foreign accent. I tell him, “It’s okay,” and he smiles. This time I smile back. I keep walking, wondering what those interactions meant, if anything. I can feel my father today. He is with me somehow, but it’s hard to explain. I even find myself swinging my arms like he did when he walked.

I stop to sit on my usual bench in Dupont Circle, sip from my water bottle, and watch the people I call the randoms. They are homeless, or live in shelters or halfway houses, I guess. Some are mentally ill but very high-functioning. There’s a guy with an old transistor radio he carries around. He talks into it, as if he’s communicating with someone in another dimension. There’s a girl who’s maybe in her early twenties with stringy hair and a mean mouth. She smokes the ends of cigarettes she finds on the ground and is always dancing around like a child who needs to go to the bathroom. There’s a guy in a cowboy hat busking with a guitar, always smiling no matter who’s listening. There are some people who have given up on any kind of shtick, dirty Dunkin' Donuts coffee cups on the sidewalk in front of them. There's a woman who puts on a daily one-act play for herself. She's very committed, even without an audience. She cries on command, and her voice has this quaver that's really authentic. She's been doing the same material for a while now. It involves a grandmother, who is an empty water bottle with what looks like real hair taped to it, and a couple of holes jabbed into the plastic for eyes. Today, she actually has an audience, but it's the skinny guy with greasy hair who sleeps standing up. When she finishes, she points across the park to someone they call the sailor. Sure enough, the guy's wearing a sailor's hat. She tells the skinny guy it's a story he made up, that he never sailed around the world, that the guy's never seen a boat. The skinny guy starts giggling.

I've watched them all for months. Yes, I was given a raw deal, but I could be brushing my teeth in a public fountain with a used toothbrush, or putting on a one-act play of gibberish to a one-man sleeping audience. Still, I'm waiting for the physical weight of my father's absence to lift. It's something I carry around, like a metaphorical backpack full of stones.

While I'm out, Jenna calls from some house in the

Hollywood Hills owned by her mother's friend. She's doing an internship in PR for film. She'll be great at it. She can talk to anyone, and she's beautiful. She looks like she could be the daughter of Halle Berry. She started dreadlocks a couple years ago, so they sort of sprout out of her head at different lengths and angles. She is the queen of social media, constantly posting pictures that I usually duck out of.

"T, I can't wait for you to get out here. There's a pool boy!"

"Wow. But, Jenna, I'm not exactly the Hollywood type."

"Girl, you are all that and a bag of Cheetos. You just need a little nudge."

When I first started hibernating in my room, Jenna was the only one I'd let in. She'd come over to fix my hair or show me some special eyeliner, and she'd bring pistachios, which was all I'd eat. Her visits were the only thing that temporarily cheered me up. She's super fashionable, whereas I'm the girl who puts her hair in a ponytail and calls it a day. When we're out together, she looks like the pop star and I look like the assistant.

"Whatever. I have to work on these stupid college applications."

Jenna makes a noise on the other end. It's a sore subject.

She wants me to rejoin the swim team next year, so I can get into a good school. She's very college focused, and I'm, well, I don't really know what I am. She's right, though, I would need swimming to get into a top school. My grades are average. I used to get A's, but my father dying didn't exactly boost my GPA.

"Anyway, when you come, you can show off your swimming talents for the pool boy."

I'm blushing, thankful no one in the park can see me or even cares. "We'll see."

"Well, wish me luck. I have my first day today. I've changed outfits like a hundred times."

"Jenna, you could wear a paper bag and look hot."

"Thanks, T! I think I'll keep you around forever."

"I'm not sure how long any of us will be *around*."

"T, don't be morbid."

"Okay, have a great day. I'm sure you'll kill it."

"Thanks. Get those college apps done so you can get out here, okay? I miss you!"

"Miss you, too."

I hang up and head home. The sun has slipped behind some clouds, cooling down the air a little, and people's moods seem to be elevated as well. The smiling continues. I think of my father, and try to smile back.

When I get home, the house is completely silent except for the ticking grandfather clock at the bottom of the stairs. Mom is probably at yoga, and Larry is still at work. I grab some yogurt and plop down on the living room couch, turning on the TV. It's tuned to local news. I start to change the channel, but the meteorologist woman is smiling so widely, it's infectious. Like one-hundred-degree weather is the happiest thing in the world.

After the weather, they do a "breaking news" segment on a guy who was killed in Columbia Heights when some scaffolding collapsed. They cut to people talking about what a great person he was, then his mother crying, then other neighbors saying they're concerned about safety with all the construction in our city. I don't think twice about it, but then the victim's name comes on the screen: *Brady Hart.*

I run to the kitchen and get the box of Cheerios out of the trash. The name is still there, underlined. *Brady Hart.*

I feel my heart leap as I release my grip, and the box falls to the floor.

2.

there are no coincidences

Sleep has been one thing that comes easy for me, pulling me into an empty state, a beautiful nothing where I don't have to think. It's when I wake up that the harsh reality settles in: *My father is no longer on the planet.* But this morning, it's that man's name that first enters my mind. It doesn't make sense. How could a dead man's name be underlined on my cereal box? What is going on?

I get out of bed, put on my swimsuit with some jean shorts on top, grab my bag, and walk the four blocks to the community pool. The dour woman who sits at the front gate is reading a self-help book. She gives me a quick nod and lets me in.

It's nice to be here this early, before the buses full of day campers come and the whole atmosphere becomes chaotic. It's quiet, and the water is sleek and bright, unruffled like a perfectly pulled sheet. I throw my towel on a nearby chair and start stretching. I'm thinking about the red-haired woman, the boy, and the man with the thick accent. They were strangers, but I felt connected to them. As if they really *saw* me. For so long I've been lost, unseen, kind of sneaking through my days, but yesterday was different.

I pick the far lane, close to the lifeguard, whom I've barely noticed before. He has bleached hair and, like, a sixteen-pack. He smiles at me in a flirty way. I attempt to smile back, but he's already waving at someone else.

I step into the water, twirl my hair up, and stuff it underneath my cap. I dunk my head. The water is cold. I'm suddenly self-conscious, even though I'm in a one-piece. The other fast girl on the swim team, Gwendolyn, once told me my nose was big and my swimming cap accentuates it. When I told Jenna, she said, "Damn, here I was thinking Gwendolyn was the *good* witch."

I adjust my goggles, take a deep breath, and go under. I push off hard, swimming most of my first lap underwater. I feel clean in the pool, the water filling every pore of my skin. I emerge in a full freestyle, alternately breathing on each side. My arms break the surface, my breath like a delayed heartbeat, my body a precise and unrelenting machine. I go into a deep pocket of time, and the water becomes an escape, a way to make sense of a world that doesn't make sense to me right now.

Swimming has always been my thing. Coach Dawson, who I've always just called *Coach*, said that I could easily win regionals, then nationals, and eventually try out for the Olympics. When I walked into his office and told him I was quitting, his eyes filled with tears. He told me he understood, and that his door was always open to talk. A couple times when I was overwhelmed, I took him up on it. He told me about also losing his dad when he was a kid and showed me his picture. Another time, he helped me by doing this super annoying math homework. I knew he wasn't supposed to do my work for me, but after losing someone close to you, the usual rules go out the window. He did it, and I accepted it, and I was thankful to have one less thing to worry about. It's the little gestures that carry a lot of weight. Like the day he told me I'd always have a spot on the team. But after everything that had happened, I lost my competitive spirit along with part of my heart.

Today, though, I feel like I could swim circles around Gwendolyn, my big nose and all. I flip, turn, and push off, rocketing through the clear blue, suspended in a kind of liquid gravity. When I come up for air, I can hear the world going on, in aural fragments—a car horn, a faraway voice—but it's the water I crave, where I can be completely immersed, cut off from the world and shut into my thoughts.

I gain momentum as my mind goes back to the summer after freshman year in Rehoboth Beach. My father had a cottage there, in the woods, about a mile off the shore. He took me sailing, and we'd eat peanut-butter-and-banana sandwiches on the boat, with nothing around us for miles but the shimmering ocean. "Everything tastes better out here," he'd said, and he was right. He'd sing these silly Irish songs and pretend he was a drunk pirate. It never got old. We'd get giant Slurpees on the boardwalk, chase pigeons, and secretly laugh at the old ladies with blue hair and eyebrows drawn in the wrong place. We'd get up early and go for lemon pancakes at the diner, and then look for purple shells on the state beach. I never felt inferior around him. I was the center of his world. He told me I could be whatever I wanted to be. All I want now is to be a girl with a father who's alive.

After twenty laps, I stop for a break and catch my breath. The earlier lifeguard has been replaced by a middle-aged guy with a small ponytail and a potbelly. He waves at me awkwardly.

I start again with the breaststroke, letting the water rush past my face before each intake of breath, plunging back in, anticipating the dip and curve of my neck. Swimming is all about the rhythm and the timing. Dive, swish, carve, pull, kick, shoot. The water is something to conquer and it feels natural to do so.

Like a GIF or a looped drumbeat, my mind goes back to the name on the box and the guy who died. Every lap is a question. If Larry and Mom didn't do it, who did? Our cleaning lady sometimes brings her little boy, maybe he underlined the letters? Was it meant for me to see? Is someone trying to tell me something? If so who and what?

When I'm finished with my laps, I dry off and go to the changing room, which smells like chlorine and mildew. There's a mirror with one large crack down the center. I look at it, positioning myself so the crack goes right through the reflection of my body. It seems fitting. I can't help but wonder if I'll ever be whole again.

Behind me, a mother tries to get her toddler's swimsuit off. The child jumps around, avoiding the mother's grasping arms, and it makes me giggle. I used to be the same way.

I stop for iced tea at Peregrine on my way home. The man behind the counter doesn't smile. I know the feeling.

I lost my smile about a year ago. Still, I try one on. He's not impressed.

I make it to our modest row house off Logan Circle, in what's known as the "gayborhood." There are lots of guys with silver crew cuts and ripped arms wearing sporty clothes and carrying little dogs. My mother runs a nonprofit and is a self-declared social butterfly. She has a lot of gay friends, including our neighbors, a couple both named Jason who we call "the Jasons," but they haven't been around much since Larry came into the picture. I don't blame them. Sometimes it's hard to believe my mother and I are even related. When I walk in, she seems ecstatic that I've already been up and out.

"Tee Tee!"

"Mom, please don't call me that."

"Well, it's nice to see you!"

She seems especially peppy this morning, probably the result of several espressos.

"Nice to see you, too, but I'm only dropping off my stuff."

"Okay! Where are you going?"

I don't have an answer, so I say the first thing that makes sense. "To see Coach."

"Oh." My mother's face twists with hope, and I have

to look away. There's no filter on her facial expressions. "That's great. Say hi for me."

"Sure."

I hang my swim bag at the bottom of the stairwell and head back out. It's not oppressively hot yet, but I can feel it coming. I have to tell someone about the cereal box, and Coach seems like a good candidate. He carries his grandfather's lucky handkerchief to swim meets, and one time, he said he *saw a sign* that we would win, and we did. He might not think I'm losing it.

I grab a hot dog from a stand that is opening and eat it on the way. It tastes fluffy and salty and juicy all at once. After I'm finished, I feel like I could eat another one. I can't remember the last time I was even hungry. There is definitely something happening to me. Maybe my mother could sense it.

I text Coach, and he texts right back to meet him at the S Street Dog Park. Technically, you're supposed to cc parents when a student texts a teacher, but Coach and my mother have known each other for years, and he's also a family friend. I zigzag the streets packed with multicolored row houses that line the brick sidewalks. This area is mostly gentrified, except for a few properties that have not been attended to in what seems like decades.

At the park, I do the double-gate dance to get inside. There's a gay couple with a blond Frenchie that has a pink, diamond-studded collar, an old man with an even older black Lab, and in the far corner is Coach, with his pug named Julie.

Julie jumps on me in greeting, and Coach says, "No jumping!" He reprimands his dog like the kids on his swim teams.

The dog is so blissfully happy, I wish I could channel her cluelessness about the world. Being a dog would be so much easier. I love Julie. Once, when I was in my deepest state of sadness, Coach brought her to school. He let me sit with her in his office while he coached the boys' team. She looked at me with such pure, unconditional love that I started to cry. Then she tilted her head and whined, and I laughed. How thin the line is.

"Hey, stranger," he says.

"Hey, Coach."

His bald head glistens in the sun. He's one of those men who shaves his head because his hair's receding. He says it's for swimming, but I think it's also for vanity. He wears a navy-blue tracksuit and an old-school green headband. Somehow he pulls it off.

"What's going on?" he prompts.

We sit on one of the circular benches. I haven't seen him

in a while, so at first it feels odd. To cover the silence, I start talking. I tell him about a book I've been reading, then ease into seeing the name and the news about the guy who died. Thankfully, I was right. He doesn't judge me. Instead, he seems a little intrigued.

"Do you think someone's trying to tell me something?" I ask.

"Could be. This has caused a shift in you. I can see it."

"I just ate a hot dog and loved it."

"What?"

"Nothing."

Julie starts barking at the Frenchie.

"Julie, no barking!" Coach yells, then turns to me. "Do you feel different?"

"Yes. Kind of."

"Well, I know you, Tegan. Whether it's a coincidence or not, you're someone who will go with her gut. That's all we can do, right? There are things happening out there that are so much bigger than us. Be careful."

Julie starts jumping around the Frenchie, who snorts and lies down, like he can't be bothered.

"Now, can we talk about you joining the team in the fall?"

"Coach..."

"I know, I know. But the team isn't the same without

you. The pool even looks sad." Coach's lower lip sticks out, beseeching me. I stare right back at him, neither a yes or no in my expression.

"Think about it?" he prods gently.

"Okay."

"And keep me posted if you get any more signs of soon-to-be dead people. Just make sure it's not me."

"Coach, you'll probably live until you're a hundred."

"I would like to live long enough to see you compete in the Olympics. How about that, Tegan?"

"Coach!"

"Sorry, sorry. Your times were fantastic. I'm sure they still are."

"Probably. I did laps this morning. I'm just not ready..."

"It's cool, I get it. Sports aren't our whole lives. You've been through a lot. But I gotta tell you, I know how much the old Tegan loved swimming. She would show up to practice early and stay late. The whole team looked up to her."

"Except Gwendolyn."

Coach waves the thought away as if it's an annoying fly.

"Forget about her. She's fast, but you're faster. You're my torpedo. I tell you what. When and if you're ready, text me when you go for your laps. I'll time you, for fun, no commitment. Deal?"

I think about it. It's hard to keep telling him no.

"Deal."

His face beams again. We hug, and I know it's weird, but I want to hang on to him. I want some kind of father figure in my life to make the world feel safe again. But when we break away, I get a sinking feeling. Coach is great, but he could never replace my father. No one ever could. I say bye to Julie, who is now sniffing out the old Labrador.

As I walk home, I think about how I've been blind since my father's death. In addition to making myself invisible, I've been moving through time and space without really connecting with anyone. Now it's as if someone turned the lights on the world. I can see everything, everyone more clearly. The patterns of the trees against the sky, the rusted wheels of locked-up bicycles, the couch in the old dumpster with its guts falling out, the toddler with a lollipop bigger than his head, the white-haired man carrying a cello on his back. I see it all and take it in, even smiling at strangers.

If I'm going to get another sign, I need to be ready.

3.

there will be ones that get away

In my dream, I'm in a helicopter with my father, but we're not in a war zone. It's a tropical landscape. There are lush green mountains, crashing waterfalls, and searing rainbows. The world is overly saturated with color and teeming with life. We're smiling at each other, and the sun is huge in the sky, shooting razor-thin rays between us. He has one hand on the controls and one hand in mine. He says something to me, but I can't hear him over the sound of the propeller. We get close to the side of a mountain, but I'm not scared because he's totally in control. We dip into a utopian valley, and for a second, I think we're going to crash into a teal-colored river, but he scoops us up at the last second. We steady out and head straight toward the horizon. Then his face turns serious, and he jumps into the back seat. "Your turn!" he yells. "Go for it!" I laugh as if he's kidding, but he's not.

I get into the pilot's seat and grip the controller with both hands. Then I look back, and my father's gone. I try to keep the helicopter steady, but I have no idea what I'm doing. I call out for my dad, but he's nowhere. All I can see is white. I release my hands and close my eyes. The propeller sound gets louder and louder. I scream, but nothing comes out.

When I wake, sweat rings the collar of my T-shirt. I immediately take a shower, trying to wash away the dream, but it leaves me with a hollow feeling. What does it all mean? I remember someone telling me that you are everyone in your dream. So I wonder if I was my father, trying to tell myself something. But that doesn't really make sense.

I dry off, put on my robe, and walk to the window to stick my hand out for the temperature. (I prefer an actual test as opposed to a weather app.) When I pull it back in, my breath catches in my throat. There's a name written in the dust on the windowsill.

tom elliot

I jump back a little and stare at it, frozen in shock. I can almost hear my heart pounding through my chest. I blink twice to make sure I'm not seeing things, but it's still there. I frantically wipe it away, but the letters are seared in my mind. *tom elliot.* My stomach flips over itself, and at that moment, I feel alive. My blood runs as if someone plugged me into a charger. I literally *leap* to my desk and open my laptop, typing in the name. There are five Tom Elliots in my zip code. To get their phone numbers and addresses, I use the credit card my mother gave me for emergencies. I'm pretty sure this counts as an emergency. I start to make a list, but then I crumple it up and throw it away. What am I even doing?

I try to distract myself with a podcast, but it doesn't work. I take the list out of the trash and uncrumple it. I stare at the creased letters, shaking my head. I can't sit here; I have to do something, so I start calling the numbers. A woman answers on the first ring. I tell her I'm an old friend, and she gives me Tom's number in Utah. I cross him out. The next one doesn't answer, and the machine has someone else's name on it. I nix that one, too. The third is a nonworking number, and after that is an old lady who hangs up when I ask for Tom. She must be a widow.

This is stupid. I go back to my podcast, but again the

voices go in one ear and out the other. I keep looking at the crumpled list. All but one is crossed out. I sigh loudly, as my mother walks by my room.

"What is it, honey?"

"Nothing," I say, as if saying it will make it true. "Just going to start on my applications."

She gives me a thumbs-up and walks away, like that's totally normal. But it doesn't feel that way. I look back at the last number on the list. I plug the numbers into my phone and stare at it awhile before hitting the call button. "You've reached Lisa, Edward, and Tom Elliot," a woman says. "You know what to do."

No, I don't, I want to say. When it beeps, I hang up quickly.

I search online for their names, and an address appears in the online phone book. Dupont Circle? That's right near me. My mother comes to my room with some juice, and I quickly hide the crumpled paper.

"Thanks," I say, drinking the whole glass.

"You were thirsty, huh?" my mother says.

"Yes. Thank you."

I wait for her to leave, trying to make my face look normal. When she does, I turn to my laptop and check Google Earth. He's right on the other side of Dupont

Circle, above an old Irish pub. I find a Facebook page for him. In his profile picture, he looks my age, maybe a little older. His last post was four months ago. His Instagram is private.

What do I have to lose? I'm either crazy or I'm not. I dress and sneak out of the house, managing to avoid Larry and my mother (an advantage of the master bedroom being on the third floor). I have no idea what I'm doing, but I feel magnetized, as if some force is pulling me. When I arrive at Tom's, I wait outside his house for the better part of an hour, avoiding eye contact with some randoms who seem to appear out of nowhere: a woman carrying a teddy bear and a golf club, and an old man with a paper bag covering a large bottle of beer.

When the person I recognize as Tom Elliot finally comes out, he takes a left and walks, head down. It looks like he's on a mission. I follow him, maintaining a short distance between us. He's dressed like a California dude—curly blond hair, cut-off jean shorts, and red Converse sneakers. The weird thing is, he's wearing a scarf in this heat. It's a light cotton scarf, but still.

He takes another left down an alley. At the end, there's a small park with what looks like old seats from a movie theater. There's trash scattered around, soda cans and candy wrappers, and a large tree with a tiny tree house that looks half-built. He stops in front of the tree house and places something on the top step. Then he turns to go back the way he came, by where I'm standing. I duck out of the way so he can't see me. My breath quickens and sweat beads on my temple, which I wipe with the sleeve of my T-shirt. I pretend I'm on my phone, facing away, but when he reenters the street from the alley, I catch a glimpse of him up close. It seems like his whole face is trembling.

When his back is to me, I run into the alley to see what he placed on the top step of the tree house. It's a rock. On it in red marker, it says:

E—

I'm sorry.

—T

I pick it up. It's warm, as if it had been in his pocket for a while. I put it back and run to catch up to him. At first I don't see him and think about going home and forgetting all this nonsense. But when I look down the street, I see his scarf in a cluster of people waiting for the light to change on Pennsylvania. I make it to the corner and wait. I look at my hands. They're shaking. Like the moment before a bomb goes off, or the second before a giant wave flattens a village. I know it's coming. But what?

When the walk sign comes on, Tom picks up his pace and so do I. Eventually he hops onto the escalator at the mouth of the Dupont Circle Metro station. I take a different escalator and stay about ten steps behind.

There are about twenty people on the platform, all waiting patiently for the train, some on their phones, some reading the newspaper, some staring into space. Everyone is pretty much stationary. Except Tom Elliot.

As I hear the train approaching, he breaks into a run and jumps off the platform right as the train pulls in.

You could almost call it graceful. His body unfurls in the air as he leaps off the edge, seemingly in slow motion, his scarf waving behind him in an arc. There's a strange, elongated second of beauty before impact. I watch in complete horror. A collective gasp echoes through the station, like when an athlete shoots but misses at a sports game. The train's brakes are high-pitched and piercing. It pulls to a stop, and for a second, it's completely silent. Then a child starts to cry.

It hits me like a punch in the gut.

I could have done something.

Was I supposed *to do something*?

I am too late.

The child wails louder, and people are making a commotion, dialing 911. There is blood on the platform and on the tracks. Many people start to flee the scene, as if they don't want their lives touched by such atrocities. But others walk closer, peering over the edge at what death and destruction look like.

I stand there, unable to move, until what must be a while later when the EMTs carry the body away in a green bag.

When Tom walked out of his building, he was focused. At the tree house, he seemed afraid, maybe sad or angry. But weren't most people? Is that how wafer-thin the line is between living and not living? A line that one can cross in a split second? The two people whose names I saw died on the same day. Should I tell Jenna or my mother? They'd think I was seriously losing it. Maybe I am.

I walk to Coach's apartment in a daze, but he's not there. I text him that I need to see him, and he texts back that he's in Virginia visiting his mother, but he'll see me on Saturday.

I go home and try my best to avoid Larry and my mother, although they can tell something's up. My body is still shaking.

"How was your day?" my mom asks.

I can see the jump replaying in my mind, and feel the powerlessness, like when you drop something and you see the impact coming, knowing it's going to break.

"Fine," I say. As I turn to leave, I knock over Larry's coffee mug, and it shatters on the floor. "I'm sorry!" I start to pick up the shards, and cut my finger.

"Whoa, whoa, hold on," Larry says, wrapping my finger in a paper towel. "I'll clean that up."

"Honey, is everything all right? What's going on?" My mother has that super concerned look on her face, like the time I had chicken pox. I'd looked in the mirror and was so scared. I was covered in pox. She took me to the doctor, and when we got home, she lay with me that whole first night, never leaving my bed.

"I'm not feeling well," I manage to say.

Larry methodically picks up the pieces, holding my finger. "It's okay," he says. "When I was in college, I'd walk into the bar and everyone would grab their drinks."

My mother laughs, and it feels off, as if she's only trying to please him.

My mom hands him a Band-Aid, and Larry wraps it around my finger. It's the first thing I've ever seen him do that's useful.

I excuse myself and head upstairs to my room and lie on my bed, staring at the ceiling. Is this really happening to me? What on earth made Tom do that? And what about the rock he left at the tree house? Who was *E*?

I remember when I found out my dad died. It was as if the earth beneath me was no longer solid, like my knees could buckle and I could melt into a puddle, like everything was sucked out of me. I had nothing. But even then, suicide was never an option. I didn't want my life without my dad, but I didn't want to die. I didn't think I had the courage. I wonder now if it is courage or cowardice?

My mother comes in to check my finger. I don't let her look at it, saying it's fine. She flips through the college brochures on my desk. I can tell she wants to say something, but am grateful she doesn't.

When she leaves, I'm too exhausted to think about anything. I fall asleep in my clothes.

I never remember my dreams, but ever since the helicopter one with my father, I'm starting to. Tonight, I'm on the escalator at the Dupont Circle Metro, and Tom is behind me instead of running ahead. I get off first, ready to block him. I try to get his attention when he reaches the platform. He has the same expression as in the alley. That trembling face. I start yelling, but he doesn't hear me. I hold out my arms. The train is speeding into the station. A child is laughing. He runs right through me.

He leaps, and I reach for him. I grab his scarf. Tom gets squashed by the train, and I am left holding his scarf.

....

The next day I swim most of the morning, still not able to get the image out of my head. Tom's body unraveling in slow motion, the undulating scarf, the blood on the platform. The dream in which I couldn't save him.

I'm grateful for the water. It's all-consuming. I lose myself in my focus, quelling the boiling pot of questions in my head. I use my legs to kick, my arms to slap, push, and pull. I duck fast to flip, savoring the escape of being fully submerged. The pool always gave me purpose. But now it feels bigger than that, bigger than improving my times, bigger than me.

After I finish, dry off, and change, I decide to walk back to Tom's apartment building. I don't have a plan, so I sit on the shaded stoop, waiting for a sign. A random comes up and asks me for change. She has on a GWU sweatshirt with holes in it and carries a greasy bag of old french fries. I shake my head.

Then a man leaps up the stairs, paying no attention to me, and rings the doorbell. He's clearly distraught. He must know what happened. *What if it's Tom's father?* I will myself to stay put. If I can find something out about Tom, maybe it would explain why I was chosen to see his name. *Chosen.* It sounds so *hocus-pocus,* as my mother would say.

The man rings the bell, but no one answers.

"Excuse me," I say, but it doesn't sound like my voice. I never talk to people I don't know. But then again, I never get advance notice someone's going to die. "Are you here about Tom?"

The man looks ragged, but his nice clothes create an illusion of togetherness. "He is…was my nephew. Did you know him?"

"No. Yes. Well, sort of."

"Were you his girlfriend?"

"No." I don't tell him I've never been anyone's girlfriend, or that two of the boys I kissed in middle school are now gay.

"Well, what are you doing here?"

"I don't know," I say. I can't tell him about seeing Tom's name on my windowsill; it would sound too weird. "I guess I'd like to pay my respects, you know…"

"Of course," the man says, handing me his phone. "Put

your number in my contacts. I'll let you know when the service is. I just flew in from Charleston. I think it's on Friday. I don't know where my sister is. We're all in shock."

"I know," I tell him, "I'm so sorry." My fingers tremble as I type my number into his phone. When I hand it back, he looks at the screen and says, "Tegan."

"Yeah. What's your name?"

"People call me Rex." His eyes flick around, and he makes a weird groaning sound. "You can't trust anything anymore."

"I know."

"I need to find my sister," he says quickly. His voice catches. "We had no idea. There was no explanation..."

"Yeah, I know."

"What?"

"My...my father was in the military. He was killed in Syria." Again, my voice sounds like someone else's. I can feel blood rushing to my head. I grab onto the railing to steady myself.

"Oh, I'm so sorry."

"I don't know why I said that. *I'm* sorry. I mean, I'm sorry for you. For Tom."

I stand up straighter, and Rex hugs me. I am not a hugger, but it feels good to share my grief with this stranger. When we separate, I think he's going to ask who the hell I really am. But he closes his eyes and sighs. It's not a sad sigh. It's a world-weary sigh, and it reminds me of my father. I look up at the clouds. I try to feel him. I think I do.

Rex says a quick goodbye and takes off. I stay on the stoop for a little while, still not sure what I'm waiting for, until a woman comes. She has been crying. She's alone. Her hair is frizzed out, and she's carrying a bag of oranges.

"Are you Tom's mother?" I ask as she starts up the steps.

She looks terrified for a second, then her face softens, but the fear doesn't leave her eyes. "Yes, who are you?"

"I knew Tom." I know it's a lie, but it feels like I've stepped on a moving walkway and it's too late to get off.

"Oh, oh, come in," the woman says, handing me the bag of oranges and getting out her keys. "Please, come in."

I wonder if I should be doing this. What if she figures out I didn't even know him? Should I tell her the truth? We go inside and sit on her couch. Before I can come clean, she starts sobbing, her head slumping forward. There is nothing I can do but comfort her.

"It's okay," I say, knowing that's a stupid thing people say. "Actually, it's not okay. But it's not your fault."

The woman stops crying and stares at me, as if trying to come up with some reason I'm sitting on her couch. I don't have one, but I also know that I shouldn't be anywhere else. That right now, my life is about being here. In *this* moment.

"I was there," I tell her. "It was quick. And this is going to sound weird, but it was kind of beautiful."

"What?"

Her face twists into a grotesque shape. She starts crying harder, and it's so heartbreaking that I do, too. After a while, we calm down and just sit together. Soon, some relatives come over, and they don't even ask who I am. They barely say anything, simply take their turns comforting Tom's mother.

Then a girl comes over. She looks cold and sullen. She's wearing a bikini top and shorts, and her hair is greasy. I hear one of them call her Sam, and my heart starts racing. Is she his girlfriend? She'll blow my cover.

I try to sneak out, but Sam blocks me in the hallway.

"Who are you?"

"No one," I say.

She looks at me with dead eyes, her expression blank. "What are you doing here, then?"

"It's a long story."

She snorts and says, "Do you go to Westville?"

"Yeah," I lie.

"Well, Tom went to Dale Ridge. Nice try. I've never seen you before. Why are you here?"

"Look, I can explain how I know Tom, but I'll sound…"

"You'll sound…what?"

"What's going on out here?" It's one of the women who has been comforting Tom's mother. Maybe an aunt. She has bleached hair, and her mascara's running.

"Nothing, I was just leaving. Sorry again, for your loss."

"Sorry for yours," Sam says, and lets me pass, but not without giving me an *I'm on to you* look.

On my way home, I can't get Sam's face out of my head. I wonder how she knew Tom. The thing is, I feel the loss, too. I saw it happen. I could have done something. I could have talked to him in the alley, at the tree house, at the stoplight. Somehow, I could have changed his mind. I remember my father telling me that helping people is the best thing you can do in life. But it feels like I was given the chance and failed.

I leave a short while later and stop at the alley by the tree house. It all seems different from before. I check the top step, and the rock is still there. When I touch it, it's cold. I shiver, turning to head home.

I run up the stairs to my room when I get there, and start working on college applications to get my mind off the whole thing. I get as far as filling in my name and address. Then I call Jenna, but I'm not really in the conversation. I want to confide in her, but it feels pointless.

That night, I dream of Tom again. This time, I grab the scarf and pull, and his body comes with it. I'm able to drag him back onto the platform a millisecond before the train comes. We stare at each other as everyone gets on the train. Then Tom runs away, up the escalators. Again, I'm left holding his scarf.

....

In the morning, I swim laps, then go to my favorite museum. It's quiet on the third floor with the impressionists. I sit on a bench for a while as people come and go, each with their own ambitions, hopes, and dreams. Some of them look bored, some wide-eyed and full of wonder. A woman in a sari, and older man in a bow tie, two Korean girls about my age: I notice all of them. Even though I feel lost, I'm grounded by the bench in this room. One of the security guards asks if I'm all right. He has blue-black skin and a big smile.

"Not really," I tell him.

"Do you want to talk about it?"

I look at him closely. His brown eyes are kind. There's a small scar on his cheek in the shape of a comma.

"Can I tell you without you making judgments?"

"Try me," he says.

"Do you ever feel like you've been chosen to do something? Something that's beyond your control?"

He looks confused, but then his face softens.

"You mean like, doing what your heart tells you as opposed to what your logical brain tells you?"

"Yes."

"That's the human condition," he says, like it's the simplest concept in the world.

"Hmm," is all I can say.

"Nine times out of ten, I'd go with your heart—but that's just me."

"Life lessons from a security guard."

He laughs. "You take care, young lady, and be safe."

"I'll try."

I watch him walk out of the room. At the doorway he turns back and smiles again, and so do I.

Another name could come. I keep looking, but nothing happens. Maybe that was it. Maybe that was my only chance and I blew it. But I still have that feeling. Something is happening. This is only the beginning.

....

On Friday, I try to figure out what to wear to Tom's service. I decide on one of my mother's shift dresses, because it's simple and not too flashy.

On my way, I check the tree house at the end of the alley again. My jaw drops when I see the top step. The rock is gone. Whoever it was meant for must have picked it up.

The church is packed with people, and I try not to make too much eye contact. After a couple hymns are played, a few family members get up and talk about what a nice boy Tom was. It's unbearably sad to see everyone crying, but also strangely comforting. I feel like screaming, *I know this feeling!*

Afterward, as we all file out, Tom's mother hugs me like she's always known me. I can see Sam in a black dress a few feet away, smoking and staring at me, shaking her head. I smile and wave at her, but her expression stays the same: hard, cold, almost calculating. She walks away by herself. Partway down the block, she turns again, and I look at my feet so she doesn't catch me staring at her.

When everyone's gone, off to the graveyard with the casket, I go back inside the church. It's cool and dark and feels peaceful now that it's empty. I think about how many tears have been shed here, how many desperate prayers for people facing death, hopelessness. How do you make sense of it all?

I check for another name in the wood walls or the stained glass, but instead, I see a person sitting in the front pew. I get closer. It's a boy, around my age, maybe a sophomore. He's got on those cool red headphones. I wait in the aisle for a minute before inching down his row.

He's listening to hip-hop, or maybe EDM. I can hear the tinny beats secondhand. I can't tell if his black hair is super styled or not at all. He turns. His eyes are like green arrows shooting into mine.

"Hey," I say, though I know he probably can't hear me.

He pulls one headphone off. His cheekbones are sharp.

"Hey back," he says, deadpan.

"What are you doing?"

"What does it look like?"

"Did you know Tom?" I ask.

"No, I just go to the funerals of strangers."

I laugh abruptly, and he gives me a weird look.

"I'm Tegan." I reach out my hand, shaking his firmly, like my father taught me to.

"Edge."

I sit next to him. He puts the headphone back on, and we stay like that. Two lone kids in an otherwise empty church. I should leave, but wait for what happens next.

4.

take the chance

He listens to his music, and I listen to my thoughts.

The church is completely silent aside from the muffled beats from his headphones.

Eventually he slides one headphone off again, revealing his ear, which is kind of cute, if ears can be cute.

"Why'd he do it?" I ask.

A thin smile sweeps across Edge's face, and it strikes me that maybe he's an imposter, too.

I have this theory that at some point, we all reach a boiling point and become distilled. That's what I feel like now. Can he see me—like, really see me?

He takes off the other ear so the headphones curl around his neck like a giant red necklace. "Why do *you* think?"

"I don't know. I didn't...I didn't know him."

"I didn't either, really."

"So you *do* go to the funerals of strangers. That wasn't a joke?"

"Jokes are always half-truths. Plus, you're here, too..."

"Yeah, but I saw a sign."

He makes a noise and says, "Was this before or after the apocalypse?"

"Shut up. You won't believe me anyway."

He pretends to be nonchalant, but his left eyebrow rose a little when I said the word *sign*.

"Try me," he says.

A maintenance person with a scruffy beard approaches us, carrying a mop. He tells us we have to leave and that he's sorry for our loss. Edge grabs his skateboard from underneath the pew, and we both scoot out of the row and down the aisle.

Moving from the dark church into the bright world is like we're being reborn into the day. Everything is sparkling: the railings, the car windows, the sidewalks. We start walking toward 14th Street. Heat comes off the sidewalk in visible waves.

"I hate when people say 'sorry for your loss.' All of the sayings are bad, but that one's the most generic."

Edge isn't talking, but he's listening, so I continue.

"There's no right or wrong thing to say to console someone, but it always comes out wrong, because no one gets what it's like, unless they've experienced it themselves. Have you?"

His gets this far-off look for a second, and then he says, "Do goldfish count?"

At first I think he's serious. Then we both start laughing. *Please be single*, I think, crossing my fingers behind my back.

"So, I'm guessing your parents didn't name you Edge."

"No. It's Edgar, but people have been calling me Edge since middle school."

"Are you gonna be a senior?"

"Junior. Eastern. You?"

"Senior. Dunbar."

We take a second to acknowledge the unspoken understanding that based on location, my school is slightly better than his, and that I'm also a grade higher.

"So who died?" he asks. We're stopped on a corner, waiting for the light to turn. It's the same corner where Tom Elliot stood, days ago. I glance at a man standing next to me and shudder. He's ghostly pale, with a long face and empty eyes. He's carrying a Bible. The walk sign lights up, and everyone starts to move.

"My father."

As we continue, the pale guy lags behind. He sways, unstable on his feet, as if he might collapse from the heat. I try not to notice he's following us, but his presence is strong. A ghost man.

"Wow. I won't say sorry for your loss..."

"But you just did."

"I know."

I shrug. I glance behind me once more, and the ghost man is nowhere to be seen. "Did you know Tom, really?"

Edge looks up at the sky, then squints straight ahead into the distance, like the answer is out there, but not in focus. He wipes a drop of sweat from his temple.

"Enough," he says. "What about you? If you don't go to random funerals, what were you doing there? What was the sign?"

We turn right at the end of the crosswalk on 14th, where a cluster of twentysomethings has gathered on the sidewalk outside of Pearl Dive, drinking happy-hour beers. We have to maneuver around three bulldogs, drooling and droopy, miserable in this heat, who are tied up, waiting for their owners.

"You're not going to laugh at me?"

"Only if it's funny."

"It's not, actually. I saw his name."

"What?"

I tell myself to stop. Here I am, hanging out with a totally cute boy. I can't ruin it by telling him what happened. I can only imagine how strange it might sound to him. I change the subject.

"How about this? Tell me one thing about yourself that most people don't know."

I had heard that on some TV show, and I feel dumb after asking it.

"Wait. Are we in therapy now?"

We walk by Ted's Bulletin. In the window is a display of gleaming donuts in long, perfect rows with sugary toppings of every color imaginable. Pink, yellow, pastel blue…

"I'll get you a donut if you tell me," I say.

"Okay. But we have to sit. It's too hot."

He leads me to a bench in the shade. When he inadvertently touches my arm, it tingles and little shock waves travel up it.

"Okay, we're sitting."

The bulldogs lope past us with their owners, tongues swinging. There's a warm breeze I turn my head into, thankful for how it feels on my face.

"I'm an alien," Edge says.

"C'mon."

"Okay, I'm not an alien. But I believe in alien life."

"And the apocalypse?"

He smiles again, and I resist the urge to move the piece of hair that has fallen in front of his right eye.

"So are you going to tell me or what?"

I think about all the time I had, between when Tom Elliot left his house and when the train came. Twenty minutes? I could have done something to save him.

The ghost man from earlier walks by, and this time he's not carrying his Bible. He's looking at his shoes. Black Crocs with socks. When he passes us, he looks back at me, giving a slight nod.

"Ugh, that guy's creepy."

"Which guy?" Edge asks.

"The old pale guy who just walked by. He's like a ghost man."

Edge looks down the sidewalk in the direction I pointed, but he shrugs. "Must have missed him."

I look down the sidewalk, too. It's empty aside from a few kids playing hopscotch. I decide to take a chance.

"Okay, I'll tell you, but first I have to get you a donut. Maybe one made by aliens."

Putting my hand on his knee as leverage, I get up to walk toward the shop.

I get a regular glazed for me, and a butter crunch for him. The guy that sells them to me says, “Cheers,” except he’s not British, so it doesn’t seem convincing.

I go back to the bench, and we both dig in. It feels so good to like food again. For so long everything tasted bland. Food was a burden. Maybe I needed someone like Edge to eat with.

“This is crazy good.”

“Astounding,” Edge says. “How did you know I like butter crunch?”

“A hunch. A butter-crunch hunch.”

He smiles again, and a warm feeling swells in my chest. I haven’t felt this content since my father died. I didn’t think it would be possible to ever feel that again. Even though I’m creeped out by the events of the past few days, not to mention the ghost man, I feel strong. Happy, even.

“I once ate only pistachios for, like, a month.”

“Did you turn green?”

“No, but my fingers were sore from constantly opening them.”

Some nannies walk by us, pushing toddlers in fancy strollers. They’re sweating, but they seem used to it. Another guy in a fishing vest carries a portable fan. We finish our donuts and throw our wrappers into a nearby trash can.

"So. Are you going to tell me about the sign now or do I have to tell you about aliens?"

"You promise you won't think I'm weird?"

He holds up his left pinkie. "Pinkie promise."

"What are we, seven?"

We curl our pinkies together anyway. I look at him. His façade is washed away, and I see something pure in his expression, like he is distilled, too.

I tell him everything, right there on 14th Street, on a bench in the shade, with barely a breeze. He listens to every word. When I finish, I ask him what he thinks.

"I believe you," he says. "One hundred percent. I'm just..."

He gets that far-off look again, and this time he might be fighting off tears. "Do you think there'll be more signs?"

"Yes."

Silence. I wonder if he can hear my heart, or if it will burst out of my chest. I close my eyes and feel a wave of fear, doubt, excitement, confusion. When I open them, the hopscotch kids run by, screeching, and I am pulled back into reality. I look at Edge. A piece of his hair has fallen in front of his left eye, and this time, carefully, I reach out and move it.

"You have intense eyes," I tell him.

"Is that a good thing?"

"I'm not sure yet, but I think so."

"I'll take that," he says.

We sit for a while, people watching, until it gets darker, the temperature finally dropping a little.

"Would it be totally cheesy if we took a selfie?" he asks.

"Yes, but who cares?" This doesn't sound like me. I never like taking selfies, but I'm so thankful he believes me, Edge could propose cliff diving and I'd consider it.

He holds up his phone, and I move my head toward his. "How about we don't smile, but try to be our normal selves."

"That's impossible."

"Try."

We look at the screen for a while, testing out our normal faces. Then he snaps the picture, and we both stare at the result.

Our expressions are not usual selfie expressions. It's sort of a candid selfie, if that's possible. We aren't smiling, but you can see in our eyes that we're happy.

We stand.

"I'm not going to say it was really nice to meet you..."

he says. "So how about, this afternoon felt good. I didn't worry about stuff for a couple hours."

"What do you worry about?"

"Stuff. I won't bore you with the details."

"Somehow I'm thinking it wouldn't be boring."

"Hey, give me your shoe."

"What?"

"C'mon, just do it."

I take off one of my sandals, and he pulls out a marker. He writes his number on the sole and hands it back. "If the number's still there when you get home, call me; if not, we'll leave it up to the universe."

I smile, and he touches my cheek, as if wiping away an invisible tear, then turns in one swift motion, jumping on his skateboard and rolling away. I watch him until he becomes a dot in the distance, then I make my own way home.

Some people give me second looks, since I'm walking with only one shoe on, the other pressed to my heart.

5.

find courage

The first thing I see when I wake up is the sandal on my nightstand, Edge's phone number written carefully on the bottom. I hold it up and stare at it, memorizing the sequence.

I don't call right away. I've watched enough TV and movies to know that's what you're supposed to do—wait. Instead, I call Jenna. She can hear a change in my voice and asks me what's up. I tell her about Edge, the funeral, and the number on my shoe.

"Wait, what were you doing at a funeral?" she asks.

"That's a longer story."

"So you're going to call him, right?"

"I guess. Not right away."

"Girl, you need to go get some. A skateboard, though? How old is he, fourteen?"

"Gonna be a junior."

"Well, maybe you should go to more funerals, because you sound the best I've heard you in a long time."

"I guess. I do feel…I don't know…different."

I walk into the bathroom, phone still pressed to my ear, and start the water for a bath. It fogs up the glass tiles that look like bricks.

"I can't wait for you to come out here to LA. Did I tell you I saw the guy from *Dexter* in the supermarket? He asked me about the melons! I also saw Heidi Klum at a coffee shop. She, like, doesn't age."

"Jenna, please don't become a name-dropper."

"Well, who are you seeing in Dupont Circle besides homeless people and wannabe politicians?"

"True."

I look at the tiles again, and as the last one fogs over, letters appear, as if someone had written in the steam. Again, I blink twice to make sure it's real and I'm not seeing things. But it's there: *the sailor.*

"Jenna, I gotta go."

"What?"

"I just… I'll talk to you later. Bye."

"Okay, make sure—" The rest of what she says is cut off.

I stare at the letters for a moment. What could it mean? I don't know any sailors, except my father. Eventually, I stop the water and get into the tub. I dunk my head, holding my breath. *The sailor, the sailor.* As I come up for air, it hits me. One of the randoms! They call him *the sailor.* I'd heard the story secondhand through the dancing girl, who was telling the one-act-play woman. The sailor claimed to have sailed around the world, but nobody believed him. It was kind of sad. Now *he's* going to die? Am I supposed to do something?

I immediately get out, dry myself off, and dial Edge as I stare at myself in the mirror. My face looks changed, but I can't pinpoint how. Could being only a day older show on my face?

He answers on the second ring. I'm breathing fast, thinking about Tom Elliot, how little time there was between seeing his name and seeing him... I don't want to see another person die, even if it's a random. Randoms are people, too. I have to do something.

Edge answers with a quick, low-voiced, "Hey."

"How'd you know it was me?"

"No one else calls me now that..." He pauses. "It had to be you."

"What do you mean, 'now that'?"

"Nothing. What's up?"

"I'm kind of freaking out. I saw another name."

"Ha! I knew it."

I tell him about the name, and who I think it is. "If there's a pattern to this, then the sailor is going to die today."

"And you know where he hangs out?"

"Yes."

"Ping me the location. I'll see you there in twenty."

"Wait, Edge. Are you sure we should do this? Maybe it's all been a coincidence. Maybe I am losing my mind."

"You're not. And if you are, I'm right there with you."

"Okay."

I meet Edge at the Georgetown movie theater, which is close to where a lot of the randoms sleep. I haven't seen the sailor in Dupont for a few days, and this is the other likely place he'd be. It's underneath a curved highway off-ramp, a section of concrete where fifteen men—and some women—sleep in elaborate cardboard houses. I start to lead Edge over there.

"So, it only said *the sailor* in your shower?"

"Yes, on the tiles, through the moisture or whatever."

"And there's no one in your house that would…"

"It's *my* bathroom. No one else uses it."

Edge makes a noise, and I say, "What?"

"Nothing. I should have guessed you have your own bathroom."

"It's no big deal," I reply, trying to tone it down.

We walk around the giant, curved concrete wall of the underpass, and the first person we see looks exactly like Jesus. We ask him if he's seen the sailor, and he points toward an alleyway across a patch of dirt and a broken chain-link fence. It's really just a space between two buildings. There's no one there, but there are stairs that lead to a rusted basement door that has what looks like bullet holes in it. This is way scarier than watching randoms in the park.

"You realize this is somewhere we could get kidnapped and have, like, our faces boiled off or something?" Edge says.

"They're homeless," I say, but I know exactly what he's talking about.

"Okay, let's go."

Being here together doesn't seem as bad, even though I hardly know him. But I'm guessing he has my back.

We enter the basement, which is huge and mostly dark, with groups of randoms in clusters. We walk slowly, arm in arm, like we're walking down the aisle at some sort of twisted wedding. I can hear someone laughing, or maybe they're crying. It's hard to tell. Someone shines a flashlight at us and I jump back. Then he shines it on his own face. It's the ghost man from yesterday. His black eyes are bulging, and he looks even paler than before. His wrinkled skin has a blueish tint now. I grab Edge and say, "Let's get out of here," but Edge pulls me back.

"It's cool," Edge says.

I close my eyes and wait. When I open them, the ghost man is gone, and Edge says, "Come on."

I look at Edge, who seems cautious but not really frightened. I can smell smoke and sweat and something really bad, like rotten garbage. There's a stained mattress in the corner, with a thin band of light from a dirty window above. We get closer and see a man lying on top of it.

It's the sailor.

I know because of his hat. It's that sailor's hat I saw him wearing across the park. I shudder and draw back a little when I see a needle sticking out of his arm. A spoon and a lighter sit on the floor next to the mattress, along with a couple of empty mini plastic bags. He seems to be unconscious. I look back to see if the ghost man's still there, but he's gone. The laughing/crying person is now whining.

"We may be too late," Edge whispers.

I tentatively touch the sailor's shoulder and move him a little. His eyes open for a second, then shut again. My heart is going double-time, and my stomach churns from the smell—is it dead animals?

"He's alive," I say.

"Probably not for long."

"What are we going to do? Should we call 911?"

"I'm guessing he has no health insurance. Let's put him on his side, so he doesn't choke on his own vomit."

"Okay. Good idea."

The sailor is a slight man, so it's easy to move him onto his side. There's a small photograph that he had been lying on top of. The picture is old and faded, but it looks like a man on a ship. I pick it up and put it right in front of his rolling eyes.

"Is this you?"

His eyes lock on the picture for a second. "Yes."

"Cool," Edge says to him. "That's great."

The sailor smiles sideways and shuts his eyes again. Edge grabs the bag of pale-brown powder and dumps it in a nearby drain.

On the way out, we walk by three guys who are sorting cans and bottles in the pool of light from what seems to be the only other window in the place.

"Hey, do you think you could keep an eye on the sailor?" Edge asks. "As in, please don't let him do any more drugs today."

The larger guy with the beard, who seems to be in charge of the whole recycling situation, looks up at me.

"Who are you two, his guardian angels?"

"Something like that."

The other two men scoff and tell us to scram.

On our way out, I trip over a broken bottle in the dark and it cuts my ankle.

"C'mon," Edge says. "Into the light."

Outside, in the space between the buildings, Edge takes off one of his socks and wraps it around my ankle. It's a small gesture, but it feels huge.

Within ten minutes, we're in the heart of Georgetown, with shoppers carrying designer bags and wearing Rolex watches, Gucci sunglasses, and pearls. How can these two worlds be that close? I always knew they were, but now it's sinking in. What really separates me from them? A couple bad decisions? Some unlucky twists of fate? Who says I won't end up like the sailor one day?

It's too hot to move in the world, and the idea of having to sit and talk about what we saw is too much, so we go back to the freezing-cold movie theater. Inside, we stand before the huge digital wall, staring at the choices.

"After seeing the sailor like that, I'm thinking…"

"The one with the dog?"

"Exactly." Edge smiles. "A feel-good family movie is the right choice after a homeless person's possible overdose."

"Agreed."

Edge gets popcorn and Peanut M&M's. He mixes them together, which sounds weird but it's really good to have little chocolate treats hidden in your popcorn. The movie is definitely the right choice—light, funny, heartwarming. For ninety minutes, we are simply two kids lost in a story. When it's over, I try to hide the streaks of tears on each of my cheeks. It's nice to cry about something other than myself or my father being gone. To cry because of joy.

On our way out, Edge says, "There's going to be a sequel where the dog dies."

I laugh, punching him on the arm.

It's cloudy now. As we walk back in the direction of Dupont Circle, he tells me he's obsessed about this documentary on alien life.

"I'm not a conspiracy theory guy or anything," he says, "but I like to believe there are other beings than us, out there. Life-forms, signs, all that stuff. I mean, you've seen three names now, right? That can't be a coincidence."

"I know. Plus, the guy with the flashlight. He seems to be appearing and disappearing." I look behind me, to be sure he's not following us. "Did you see him? In the basement?"

"No, but it was dark."

When we get to my house, I stop him short. "Wait."

"What?"

"My mom's kind of embarrassing, and my stepfather's the worst."

Edge laughs. "It's cool. My home life isn't exactly what you would call functional."

We sit on the stoop of my brownstone in the shade of the same oak tree I've stared at my whole life.

Edge gets that mysterious look on his face again. He's holding something in his hand. It's a rock, with red marker on it. I feel a tingle on the back of my neck that runs all the way to the base of my spine.

"Wait. You're *E*?"

"Yeah."

His eyes are getting watery.

"So, he *was* your friend."

He clears his throat and shakes the hair out of his eyes. "Since fourth grade."

I put my hand on his shoulder, which feels awkward, but I have to do something. Anything but say *sorry for your loss.*

He takes out his phone and shows me a text exchange from what looks like the last two weeks. It feels wrong reading it, knowing Tom is gone, but I do. First, Tom asks to meet Edge at the tree house, and Edge says he's busy, but maybe tomorrow. The next message is Edge asking, *Is everything okay?* Tom responds with an emoji face with one tear. I scroll to see the time until Edge's next response. It's two days later. He texts Tom to meet him at the tree house, with a question mark. But there's no response. That's the last text. There are tears in my eyes now, too, and when I look up, Edge is wiping his. I hand him the phone back.

He clears his throat again and sighs.

"We were tight, always. I knew he had depression. It started last year. Like, existentialist stuff. He kind of became a downer. I weaned off hanging with him for a while, and…ugh…I don't know."

"Look, what he did is not your fault. You can't carry that."

"Well, I should have done something."

"I could have done something," I say quietly.

"Same here."

"But now we're doing something. At least I think we did, today. But it might be nonsense."

"It's not, Tegan. I see…I see something in you."

I feel my face flush, and I can't think of what to say in response. This time, Edge moves a piece of hair out of *my* eyes. And then he kisses me.

I don't see stars or anything, but my heart picks up, and I feel another warm wave run through me. When he pulls back, I'm slightly light-headed.

"So there's that," he says.

"Yes," I reply. "There's definitely that."

I turn around and see my mother in the window, smiling wildly and giving me the thumbs-up. I cringe. The first time a boy kisses me for real—where it *means* something—and I'm watched by my mother? It seems cruel.

I quickly turn back to Edge. "So what about your situation? Who do you live with?" I ask to change the subject.

He seems a bit taken aback by the sudden question, but answers anyway. "My mom and my…let's say, *colorful* aunt."

"Colorful in a good way?"

"I'm afraid not."

We don't say anything for a moment.

"I need to go and do some damage control," Edge eventually says.

"What do you mean?"

"My mother. She's been dumped again. It's a revolving door of boyfriends where I live."

"Ah."

"It's funny, when she's all hot and heavy, she barely notices me, but when she's down in the dumps, she needs me there with her like, twenty-four seven."

"Well, it's nice of you to be there for her."

Edge sighs and puts the rock back into his pocket. "I guess."

He gets up and walks down the steps, stopping at the bottom stair and turning around.

"Text me tomorrow?" I ask.

"I'll show you a sign," he says, then he walks away. Again, I watch him until he's a small dot in the distance. Just to make sure he's real, and I'm not dreaming all of this.

....

When I get inside, Mom is calling up to Larry, saying, "Hurry up, sweetheart!" They're going to a charity event for my mother's work.

I wince at the word *sweetheart*, and the way her voice sounds girlish and high. Whatever Larry is, he's not a sweetheart, and my mother is not a girl. She always called my father by his first name, Graham. When Larry comes down, she goes to kiss him on his ruddy cheek, and I turn away, staring at the wood floor.

I get a large glass of water and drink half of it. When I put it down, Larry has already left, and my mother is staring at me. I hide my ankle that has Edge's sock tied around it behind my other leg.

"Where were you?" she asks, trying to sound casual, but her face gives away her excitement.

"Walking. I met this kid."

"Does this 'kid' have a name?"

"Edgar."

"Well, I look forward to meeting Edgar."

"He goes by Edge."

"Hmm. Sounds edgy!"

"Ugh, whatever, Mom."

She looks at herself in the entryway mirror, fixing her hair a little. My mother is pretty, but I wouldn't call her a "knockout" like Larry does. I try to remember my father ever calling her a name like that. They always made each other laugh, but they never really had that kind of gooey romance. Once, though, when I was around ten, I came home early from a birthday sleepover, and I found them dancing on the porch. They weren't pressed together, but they were looking at each other, smiling in a way that made me feel guilty, as if I was spying on a magical moment. I knew then how much they truly loved each other, and it was important to me to know that I was born out of that kind of love.

....

The next morning, I can't get the Sailor's face out of my head. He almost looked frozen. I remember one of my teachers telling me all human lives are significant, whether you live on the street or in a palace. I immediately text Edge, asking if he'll go check on him with me, but he doesn't respond right away. I wait for a little while, then decide to go myself.

Back at the off-ramp, it's pretty deserted. I guess homeless people get up early. I walk back to the alley and take the three steps down to the door. It still smells like dead animals, raw garbage, and cigarette smoke. I'm scared, but I have to know if he's okay. It's as if I'm back on the moving walkway and there's no turning around. I did this with Edge and I survived, why can't I do it alone?

Inside, someone sings while washing his face in a bucket of water. I walk over to the corner where the mattress is, using my phone's light. There is dried vomit on the floor next to it, and the picture is gone. I take a deep breath and let it out.

Did we save him?

I leave with tears in my eyes that I can't control. I cry for Edge losing Tom, for me losing my father, for the fact that people have to die in the first place. How could this be happening? Who is giving me this strange foresight? I was always proud to tell people that my dad saved lives. Is that why I'm seeing these names?

I text Edge again.

On my way home.

Went back. Sailor not there.

A minute later, he texts back.

Good.

I text a smiling face, and he responds with a bull's-eye emoji. I consider sending a heart, but decide on a thumbs-up. When I get home, my mother hugs me extra tight, and for some reason I don't push her away.

"What's going on with you?" she asks. I can't look at her face, so I focus on her beaded necklace, resting on her tanned clavicle.

"It's nothing I can talk to you about."

"What?" She pretends to be confused, but she knows exactly what I mean. I wish I could tell her about the names, how it's really scary not knowing why or how long it will last. How I keep seeing images of Tom Elliot sailing through the air, Edge's hand holding the rock, the sailor's queasy smile, the ghost man's quivering black eyes.

"Never mind. I'm actually thinking about joining the swim team again," I say, to change the topic, but as the words come out of my mouth, they sound real. Like I might actually mean it this time.

She seems to completely forget about my other comment. I can tell she wants to scream or jump around, but she smiles and says calmly, "That's great, Tegan. Really great."

That night, I dream I'm on the Metro, and everyone's face is a blur. But if I walk up to them and touch them, their faces come into focus. I go around and touch each person, and they are all people from my past: teachers, babysitters, swim instructors. There is a man at the end of the car. A skinny wisp of a man. I touch him, knowing who it is. Ghost Man. When his face comes into focus, his mouth opens. It looks like he is trying to swallow me. I scream and bolt upright.

My mother comes to my door seconds later, and I tell her she can come in.

She strokes my hair like she did when I was a kid, and it feels shameful somehow, but I don't resist. She tells me she's really worried about me.

"Just a nightmare, is all," I say. I want to ask her to sing to me like she used to, the song about the raindrops. But I'm way too old for that. I used to love the sound of her voice, and it always helped me fall asleep.

"Honey, what did you mean earlier, when you were saying you can't talk to me?"

"I knew that wouldn't get past you."

"What?"

"I don't know what I was thinking. I guess there are some things I can't tell you."

She looks hurt, but nods.

"Okay, okay. But if you ever need help..."

"Mom, who doesn't need help these days?"

"See, this doesn't sound like you. Is it this boy, Edge? What is it?"

"Mom, seriously. It's fine. I need to go to sleep and hopefully not have another dream."

"Well, if you do, I'm here."

"Thanks."

She kisses my forehead and leaves.

I turn off the bedside lamp, stare into the black, and

wait for sleep to come back, trying to hear her sing the song about how the raindrops were lemon drops, and the snowflakes were milkshakes. I did love that song.

6.

think of the possibilities

Coach is waiting for me at the pool. He smiles broadly when he sees me, puts his long arms in the air. “There’s my torpedo!”

A few weeks after my father died, when I was too sad to do anything, I walked over to Coach’s apartment, and he made me toast. It was a simple offering, and I remember eating it first out of courtesy, but then really liking it. We had sat on his couch, Julie curled up on his lap looking at him as he talked. He told me about the bakery where the bread comes from, and it felt nice to listen to a familiar voice. In his living room, there were framed pictures of all the teams he had coached. The one this year would be missing me.

After a few minutes of small talk, he took a picture out of his wallet. It was of a man sitting on a tractor, grinning in the sun.

"That's my dad," Coach said. "He was a pretty simple man, lived off the land. Died when I was ten."

"Do you remember him?"

"Oh yeah. He let me drive that tractor. It didn't go very fast, but it was fast enough for a kid like me."

I smiled. Coach really is a kid, still. He has that quality. Sometimes his shoelaces are untied, and his face always seems in a half state of surprise.

"But here's what. Every time I see a tractor, or go by a cornfield, I think of him, and I don't know..." Coach's eyes got a little misty. "It's comforting."

"For me it's the opposite. I'll see something, like even a guard in uniform, and I'll get a sinking feeling."

"Yeah. That'll change, though. It'll get better. I promise."

Now, while he leads me through some stretches, I think maybe he was right, that maybe it *is* getting better. That this craziness is all leading to something, that I'm becoming someone else, not just a girl without a dad.

Coach tells me about his trip to New Orleans.

"It's like, you walk into any bar on this one street, and there's tons of them, and the people that happen to be playing are the best jazz musicians on the planet. It's astounding."

"Cool."

"What about you? I was worried when you texted. Something about another sign?"

"Yes."

"What was it?"

"Coach, if I tell you about it, it's gonna make me sound batty."

"Okay, well, for now, we swim. Let's do a few warm-up laps, and then I'll time your 50-meter freestyle. Sound good?"

I nod. Coach seems really excited, and I am, too. For the first time in a while, it feels like I could really do this again. But I want to do it for me. Not for my mother, not for Coach, not for medals or ribbons (although I still have those proudly displayed in my room).

The water feels cold at first, but the key is to imagine your pores opening, letting the cold in so it actually warms you. There's no sense in fighting it. This is something Coach taught me early on.

On my practice laps, I lock into a rhythm and regulate my breathing. Like in a song, my arms are the guitar, my feet the bass, my breath the beat. But there is no voice. That is what I'm searching for.

I can see the tiny, white, dancing bubbles and notice a red plastic boat at the bottom in the center of my lane, abandoned by some kid. It reminds me of being younger, how every time my parents said we were going to the neighbor's pool, I felt this rush in my whole body. The pool was another world—a malleable, blue, sparkly world that made more sense than the real one. I can kind of understand what Edge means about aliens and other life. Sometimes this world we know is too unfair, too intense, too unexpected, to be the only one.

Swimming is more about release than resistance. Yes, you have to attack the water, but gracefully, more like seducing it to work for you, to find the sweet spot of movement and speed. After that, it's simply endurance.

I dive down and pick up the toy boat on my last warm-up lap, placing it on the edge of the pool. Coach picks it up and says, "Thanks. I lost that when I was five, been looking for it ever since."

I smile, taking a rest and letting the sun hit my face. Hot summer days like this make me want to stay in the pool forever. Coach gets his stopwatch ready. The lanes are filling up, but mine is clear. People know who Coach is, and some even know who I am. I've been in the local paper a few times. No one is going to mess with our lane.

"Okay, so like I always say: Be clear in your head. Find that rhythm and push it. When you think you've pushed all you can go, go farther. Your machine has all the right parts, make them work together. Strength and elegance."

He blows the whistle, and I'm off. It feels good, having the power and being in control. The water is silky and smooth, and my body kicks into gear like rapid muscle memory. I can kill it with freestyle. Still, my mind goes back to Tom Elliot and the sailor, and the ghost man, and if there's any connection between it all. *You're a force*, I can hear Coach say. *Faster. Faster.*

When I reach the mark, it takes me a minute to catch my breath. Coach is looking at the stopwatch, his mouth resting in an oval shape.

"What?"

"Tegan. You haven't been training, and you beat the fastest girl in the DMV by six-tenths of a second. In swimming, that's a lifetime!"

"I know, I know."

He does his little dance where he shakes his head and spins around. It's charming even if you don't know him.

"How much did I improve, you know, since I was on the team?"

"At least three seconds. What happened to you? Did you eat a lot of spinach?"

"No, I'm eating regular stuff. And seeing signs."

"Well, so am I. Your name on an Olympic placard."

"Coach, easy."

He ignores me and does the dance again. The lifeguard with the abs waves at me. I wave back.

I float on my back, facing the clear blue sky. Then I get out and dry off. We both sit on the bench near the lifeguard stand. Coach is still staring at the stopwatch, making sure it's real. Kind of like me watching Edge walk away.

On my way home, I see the ghost man, except this time, thankfully, at a distance. He's behind a window, inside the flower shop. His face looks very pale and eerie behind the glass. I can't tell if he's smiling, or making some kind of mocking, childish face. I quickly turn away. Does he even exist? Does he know what is happening to me? Should I go confront him?

I decide to keep going. I'm thinking about the fact that I broke my own record, about how I'm too scared to turn around and look back at the flower shop. I'm so lost in thought that when I reach the stoplight before my block, I take a step off the curb without looking up. A city bus speeds by, inches from my nose. I jerk back and a Chinese woman who's jogging in place comes over to me. "Are you all right?"

"I'm not sure," I tell her.

"Can I help you?"

"It's okay."

She reaches out her hand, "My name is Meili."

"I don't need to know your name." What if she tells me her name, and I see it somewhere? What if every choice I make from now on is going to affect whether people live or die? The thought is overwhelming, so much so that I feel like I could sink into a puddle on the sidewalk.

She looks offended.

"I'm a nurse. Are you dehydrated?"

"Yes, I mean no, thank you. Thanks for offering to help. I just spaced out," I say.

The woman puts up her hands in surrender, but shakes her head a little while she jogs off. The light turns. I glance back to the flower shop window and the ghost man is gone.

....

Larry is in the kitchen drinking coffee and looking at stocks on his phone. That's all he ever looks at on his phone.

I sit with my glass of water, staring into space. I can still hear the sound of the bus, so close to my face, like it rattled my brain. Meili's toothpaste breath. The ghost man making that grotesque face.

Larry looks up from his phone. "What's wrong, kiddo?"

I sigh. How could I begin to explain?

"Well, Larry, let's start with this. Do you really think an adult calling a seventeen-year-old 'kiddo' is okay?"

He laughs, but I can tell he's kind of taken aback.

"What would you like me to call you?"

"How about my name?"

My heart dips from saying *name.* Will it always be like that?

"Okay, come here, Tegan," Larry says, waving me over to show me his stocks, some pattern that means nothing to me.

"Am I supposed to be impressed?" I ask. "Because money doesn't impress me that much."

"What about strategy?"

"Better."

"Ah, wait, check this out."

He shows me a video of a toddler falling asleep while eating, which is pretty funny. I guess he does look at other stuff on his phone.

I retrieve my glass of water and drink it at the sink, then I head upstairs. The same document is still open on my laptop: the college essay I never started. I take a shower, looking at the steamy tiles, expecting another name, but there's nothing there. When I get out, the room is so steamy, I can't find my towel. I stand there for a second, until my phone dings. It startles me, and I slip to the ground, landing on my side, completely losing control of my limbs. I look at the tiles again, getting up slowly. Still no names.

The steam has cleared. I grab my phone, drying off as I plop on my bed. My side hurts from the fall.

It's a text from Edge.

I'm not only into aliens and EDM. I like food trucks too.

I send back a smiley-face emoji with sunglasses and ask him where to meet.

19th and I in twenty?

Sounds like a plan.

I actually try to figure out what to wear, which I never do. My father used to tell me to wear what I wanted as long as I felt comfortable. But it's different when going on a date. I decide on a flowy pale-blue top with black shorts that show off my butt a little. I text Jenna a selfie (so unlike me) and her wow emoji reply tells me she's impressed.

I meet Edge on the corner. This time he's got no skateboard, and he's wearing a short-sleeved, button-down shirt. Maybe he planned his outfit, too.

Along the park, the food trucks are lined up with only inches between them, creating the illusion of a wall.

"This is what's cool," Edge says. "You can travel the world in one block. I remember when Korean tacos were authentic, before Takorean became the McDonald's of street food and everything cool went corporate. But there's still some real deals. Today, we're doing Spanish."

He leads me to a truck that is all silver, with the word *Pepe* written in black.

"You've heard of José Andrés, right?" Edge asks.

"Yes," I say, even though I only vaguely know the name.

"These are the sandwiches he grew up eating, that his aunt would make in the middle of some tiny village in northern Spain."

"Sounds delicious."

"Got huge raves on Eater."

"What's that?"

"A food blog, dummy."

For some reason, Edge calling me a dummy doesn't feel bad. In fact, with that black hair, high cheekbones, and those laser-green eyes, he can call me whatever the hell he wants.

We order, and sit on some grass near the truck, our backs against a tree. Mine is a breaded chicken cutlet, but it's like, *artisan*. The opposite of a chicken nugget. It also has some kind of tangy sauce, hot peppers, and arugula. His is ham, with grilled vegetables and pesto. Both of the sandwiches are in crusty baguettes. We give each other a bite. It tastes so good, and I'm so happy to be alive and with a boy and eating something delicious and being hungry for a change. It is one of the most perfect meals I've ever had.

Then I see him again, across the park, carrying a broken umbrella.

"Look!" I grab Edge. "Do you see that man over there? With the umbrella?"

"No."

He'd ducked behind a tree.

"Ugh, I keep seeing him everywhere. Frickin' Ghost Man."

"Does he scare you?" Edge asks.

"Yes. It's creepy. Like seeing the names."

"I don't know. I'd kind of like that if it happened to me. It would be cool."

"Look, it's not cool when people are dying."

"They're dying every day," Edge says. "So are we."

"Yes, but, why are the names coming to me?"

"Maybe you're God," Edge says.

"Shut up."

I unwrap the sandwich to get the last bite, and there is a something written in small cursive on the wrapper, but it's blurred.

"Oh my God. Look." I show it to Edge.

He pours a little water on the distorted letters and they come into view.

jean

Edge holds it in front of him, letting out a small gasp.

"Wait, look at yours!"

He opens his wrapper, and there it is: another mushy group of letters. This time I pour the water, and it comes out crystal clear.

fordham

We stare at the two wrappers. People walk by with their food-truck items, smiling and laughing, going about their day. And we are holding a life in our hands. Or maybe not.

"Holy shit. Tegan, you realize someone or something is giving you extraordinary power?"

"I did swim the fastest 50-meter freestyle I ever have today."

"Oh my God. Hang on. I got a new people-finder app."

He takes out his phone, types the name and "DC" and "vicinity" into the app, and presses *find*.

Two women come up locally. There are two addresses, one on P Street and one across the bridge in Arlington. We decide to start with the one that's closest.

We get into an Uber and neither of us say anything. The driver tries to chat us up, but we don't really respond. Our minds are on one thing: Jean Fordham, and whether or not we can save her.

7.

give comfort

The car drops us off at a building that looks like apartments, but then we notice a sign atop the arch in the entryway: *The Church of Scientology.* Edge makes a noise.

"Here we go," he says.

Inside there's a half-circle desk with a woman behind it. She has granny glasses and a toothy smile. "Welcome. What can I do for you?"

"We're actually looking for someone named Jean…" I say.

The woman stands and points toward an office behind her. On the walk back, we can see into the offices on the side. People are holding silver tubes connected to a metering device. I had heard about this through the Jasons; they knew somebody in Scientology. It's called auditing. In another office, someone asks, "Do birds fly?" over and over to a man who is nodding his head every time like a robot.

I grab Edge's hand and whisper in his ear, "We need a code word, you know…if we have to get out of here."

"Okay, how about pomegranate?"

I start to giggle.

"It's my favorite fruit," Edge says, and it feels as if he's confessing some intimate detail about himself.

When we get to the office, I see her name on the door, and I tense. What if she has a heart attack while we're sitting in her office?

"Are we winging it?" I ask.

Edge nods and knocks on the door.

Jean Fordham is short and plump, and she's got a bob haircut and a no-nonsense look on her face. She doesn't smile but points to the two guest chairs in her office as if she's expecting us. We sit, and there's a silence that seems to be boiling in the air. Finally, I say, "We were wondering if you've been in any danger lately."

"Do you have any enemies?" Edge adds. "Or any health concerns?"

Now Jean smiles and holds up her hands, "Wait a second, are you FBI? You look a little young for that. Can I ask how you even came to be here? Do we have any mutual acquaintances?"

We both shake our heads, at a loss. What are we doing here?

"Well, then, let me ask you something. What's your greatest downfall in life?" She's glaring at us, almost daring us to answer.

"Losing the spelling bee in fourth grade," Edge jokes.

"My father dying," I say, to be honest.

"I see," she says, then takes off her glasses and stares at me. Her eyes seem empty. "What if I told you that you could be free of any harm that experience caused you?"

"That's kind of silly. He'll always be dead."

"But what we do here, is take control of our thoughts. In other words, you can choose to feel pain or choose to be free of it."

"Kinda like boxers or briefs?" Edge asks.

She ignores Edge and asks me if I would watch an introductory video.

Without letting me answer, she hits a button on her desk and automatic blinds come down so that the office is completely dark. A flat-screen TV behind her turns on and creepy music starts. Asteroids fly across the screen (Edge likes that part), then the music turns triumphant.

Dots appear around a map of all their churches. There's a man who looks like a lumberjack holding a monkey. Then another man, who looks like a Ken doll, starts talking about Scientology. When the testimonials come on—from the country western singer with bug eyes saying through Scientology she found "real inner peace and joy," to the personal trainer who says, "Thanks to Scientology, I'm building drug-free bodies,"—Edge and I both turn to each other and say it at the same time.

"Pomegranate."

Jean turns off the screen and tries to show us a personality chart.

"I'm sorry. This has been a mistake," Edge says.

"I tell you what. I'll give you a book, free of charge. You might be surprised at how it helps you take control of your life."

"More like give up control," Edge says under his breath, and I giggle. She hands us the books, and we thank her.

"Tell me something," she says. "How did you know my name? Where I worked?"

"Oh, I think we were looking for another Jean Fordham."

She gives us a skeptical look and says, "Well, read the book. My door's always open."

As we leave, I whisper to Edge, "Yeah, to lock us inside."

Outside, we immediately start laughing.

"That was so creepy!"

"It's a total cult," Edge says. "You have to give them all your money."

"Do you think it's her? That she's the one? She seemed pretty healthy to me."

"Apparently, you don't get sick if you're a Scientologist."

"Only in the head."

Edge laughs and pulls up another Uber on his phone.

"Let's check the other one."

Once we're in the car, Edge seems forlorn. I ask him what's up, and he tells me he's thinking about Tom.

"You know, one time in fourth grade we skipped school and stole a bunch of candy from CVS. It was my idea, but when we got caught, he took the blame. He was that kind of kid. He always had my back."

The car ascends the Arlington Memorial Bridge, and I lean my head on his shoulder.

"It wasn't your fault, Edge."

He pulls the rock out of his pocket, running it through his hands.

"I just wish I had texted back."

"I know," I say, as the driver pulls up to the address. "I know."

....

We get out. We're at a nursing home. We give each other a look, silently acknowledging that this must be the right place. Here we go again.

Inside the vestibule, there's a homemade sign stating the visiting hours that looks like it was made by a child. Edge checks the time on his phone. "We're good."

The woman at the front desk has thin glasses and a severe haircut. Edge tells her we're here to visit our auntie Jean, and she seems to buy it, handing us a notebook to sign ourselves in. She points down the hallway.

Out of earshot, I say, "She was weird."

"Look at this place."

I realize I'm still holding the Scientology books and drop them in a nearby trash can.

There are really, really, old people scattered about the common spaces. Not many of them are talking. Most of them seem to be dying, like, right now. One old man stares at me, pointing, like he's scolding me for something. For having my youth? Another woman, whose pale flesh is spilling out of her wheelchair, holds a doll with one eye, cooing to it, pretending it's a real baby. There's droopy elevator music playing, and it smells like mothballs and split pea soup.

I grab Edge's arm, and we continue down the hall. There's a door slightly open at the end. We peek in. A nurse is wetting a patient's lips with a foam brush, murmuring something followed by, "Okay, Jean?"

Edge and I turn to each other, holding our breath. It's her.

We wait in the hall until the nurse leaves. She smiles at us, and we try to act normal, but it's clear something is happening.

"What are we going to do?" I whisper to Edge.

"Wing it, as usual," he says.

We knock on the door, but we don't hear anything. Can she not talk? Is it that bad? I open the door slightly to peek in. An elderly woman is staring in our direction. Her eyelids are heavy, and she scowls, until she sees us and says, "Come on in," as if she's expecting us, like we're some kind of angels. Are we? Is this all in our minds? It feels real. A little scary, but real.

Jean's glassy eyes now stare at the ceiling, as if drawn to some higher power beyond it.

"Sit down, my darlings."

She must think we're her relatives. This isn't the first time I've felt like an imposter.

We sit on each side of the hospital bed, and she turns

her head both ways and smiles at us. It's odd, but also kind of lovely.

She points at a dog-eared book of poems by Mary Oliver on her side table.

"I love the poems," Jean says. "Each time I read them, I think different things. Words are so open to interpretation. And hers are so beautiful. Can you read one?"

There are some pages bookmarked. I find one called "Wild Geese." As I'm reading it, I'm thinking about Edge hearing the words in my voice, and I glance up at him. His face is soft, his eyes almost glowing.

After I finish, she says, slowly, "Now, what is your interpretation?"

I don't tell her that the words may as well have been going from my mouth into Edge's soul. That I've never felt closer to someone I barely know.

"Darling?"

"Umm…I think it was about feeling safe in the world. Knowing that things are bigger than you are."

Jean's eyes well with tears, and I grab her hand. Edge wipes at his own eyes with his shirtsleeve.

"You are so smart," she says to me. "You've always been so smart."

Jean closes her eyes, and I keep holding her hand.

Edge comes around and hugs me from behind. From the hallway, we would look like a portrait of a grieving family. In a strange way, it feels as if we are. A family of strangers.

After a few minutes, Jean wakes up again. She points to the foam brush, and I moisten her lips like I saw the nurse do. Then she points to the book again and says, “Another?”

I read another, and another, then Edge reads a couple. With each poem, Jean seems to be going somewhere new in her mind, someplace that makes her happy. Her smile remains. We take turns reading to her until she gets sleepy again.

A different nurse comes in and asks who we are.

Edge says we’re distant relatives.

“Oh,” the nurse says, motioning us into the hallway. “Are you sure you have the right person? Jean doesn’t have any living relatives that we know of. We have expected to make burial arrangements for her when she passes.”

“Tonight,” I say.

“Excuse me?” She turns her head to me.

“Nothing,” Edge says. “So, do you need us to sign something?”

The nurse sighs. “If there’s no next of kin, she becomes a statistic, you know?”

“Yes,” I say. When my father died, he was a statistic.

On the news they never said his name. He was lumped into some general number of fatalities. There was a service where a ton of people showed up, but I was pissed I never got to see him, that he was literally blown to pieces.

"My name is Leila," the nurse says. "Come find me before you leave?"

"Okay," Edge and I say together, then we go back into Jean's room. She's sleeping.

We both sit, the only noise the whoosh of the oxygen machine. I slowly reach out and take her hand again. It's soft and twitching a little.

"Do you think she's dreaming?"

"Hopefully, right?"

"I wish I could have held my father's hand one last time," I say. "Told him I loved him, that he was everything to me."

"But he knew that. With Tom..."

"Edge, he must have known. How long were you friends?"

"Since we were ten."

"How did you meet?"

Edge smiles. "At sleepaway camp. There was a clown the camp had hired."

"A clown?"

"I know, right? It was so embarrassing, we snuck out of the hall. We went to skip rocks on the lake..."

As Edge continues to tell the story, I get lost in the beautiful map of his face, the ridges and the colors and the way the light hits it.

"...he had smuggled in candy, and he shared it with me. He was always really generous, about everything."

"What about the girl, Sam?"

"She's trouble. She was using him to get back at another boy."

"She gave me a major evil eye."

"I don't think she even cared that he died."

Jean's breath becomes more labored.

"It's so weird to say that. He died. He died, and I could've done something..."

Edge starts to cry, like really cry, and it shocks me a little. I hold him in my arms and say, "Shhh," like my mother used to do to me. Eventually, he calms down.

"I'm sorry," he says.

"Please, please don't be sorry. I know what it's like to feel helpless."

"Yes."

Jean makes a noise, and it startles us, then her breathing calms.

"Do you think she's dying right now?" I whisper.

"I don't know," Edge says, slowly backing away from the bed.

Then she squeezes my hand and abruptly wakes up. Her expression has changed. Her eyes are wide, and there's fear in them, like a child being read a ghost story. Is she going to call us out? I try to make my face normal. Caring.

"Do you see me?" she asks.

I nod. "Yes, yes, I see you, Jean. I see you."

"I need to take the train," she says, her eyes glossing over and rolling back. "The one with the white clouds. There's a man reading the paper."

"Okay," I say. My whole body is trembling, and the words just come out. "I think you should take the train, too."

I wonder if the man with the paper is her husband. It is all so crushing, this line between life and death. Do we really go to a better place? A train with white clouds sounds pretty good. I squeeze her hand once more.

Her lips curve into a hint of that earlier smile, and she closes her eyes. I take my hand away.

We sit for a while longer, the sides of Edge's and my bodies touching. In the midst of death, I can feel how alive we are.

"Edge, thanks for being here," I say.

He nods, his face all serious now. He grabs my hand and places it on his heart. It's beating fast. I do the same with his hand so he can feel mine. We sit like that for a second, hands on each other's hearts.

"There's nothing we can do about this one," Edge says softly, and I nod.

In another room, a woman is quietly moaning.

I stand and get really close to Jean's face, ravaged with lines and saggy with age. Beneath it all, though, those two blue eyes are shining. Shining until the very end. Which must be right now.

"Goodbye," I whisper.

And Edge says, "Tegan, let's go." He doesn't want to hear her last breath. I get it.

I place the book of poems on her stomach, and move her hand over it. Then I take a picture with my phone, and we leave.

In the hall, we are like stunned animals. The nurse who wanted us to fill out paperwork calls after us, but we keep going. When we get outside, I have to hold on to Edge in order to stand upright. We sit on some swings in the yard of the school next door.

"She was definitely dying. I felt it."

"You were great with her. The poems…" he says.

"You were good at that, too, by the way," I tell him.

"You mean I have a future in poetry reading?"

"Completely."

We get out of the swings and start down the bike path. I can hear birds and distant traffic. Even though that whole experience was eerie, I feel peaceful. Something tells me she just passed. I feel a flash of gratitude, for knowing my father as long as I did, and that out of all the people in the world, he was the one who shaped who I am.

"So," Edge says, looking at his phone. "I have to do more damage control."

"Can I come along?"

A shadow washes across Edge's face.

"It's cool, you know, if you don't..."

"Look, hang on. Let's take a detour. Come."

He leads me to a little patch of grass between the bike path and the woods. We sit, and he says, "I'm going to tell you this, but not because I want sympathy. I lost my father, too."

"What?"

"He didn't die, but he left, when I was seven."

"And you haven't seen him since?"

"No."

"That's horrible."

"It's not all that bad. But my mother...like I said, she

goes through a lot of boyfriends, and this latest breakup, she's taking it really hard. And my aunt is a hot mess. Alcoholic gambler. My mother bankrolls her. So, my home life is not so..."

"Wow. Okay. What does your mother do?"

"She listens to my aunt's rants. She watches TV. She used to write books, now she writes a blog. But during these times, she gets really depressed and stares out the window. I need to be around her more."

"What does she write?"

"A blog about wine, which she hasn't really done in a while."

I don't know what to say, so I lean my head on his shoulder.

"Remember, no sympathy," he says.

"A little?"

"Okay, a little, but that's it."

I hug him full-on, and he smells like fresh-cut grass.

"Did you mow your lawn this morning?"

"No, I mow the lawn at the church in my neighborhood for extra cash."

"Wow. An entrepreneur."

"Reaching for the stars."

This time, when we part, I kiss him quickly, and he

watches *me* walk away. I know because before I round the corner, I look back. And he's there, still looking.

....

When I get home, my mother is picking out tiles with the tile guy. She's renovating the whole top floor of our house, or, I should say, Larry is. He's paying for it. At least there's going to be a hot tub on the patio, although getting into water Larry's been in is pretty gross to think about.

When the tile guy leaves, my mom is holding the estimate, and I can see the high-five-digits number.

"Mom, are you sure Larry's not running a Ponzi scheme?"

She laughs heartily, which I realize I haven't heard in a long time. At least not from something I said.

"He's not."

"But what does he do, really?"

"Investment stuff."

"Okay, we'll go with that. Investment *stuff*."

"How's Edgar?"

"He's good. Taking care of his mom."

"How sweet!"

"Kind of."

"Soooo…I ran into Coach at Whole Foods, and he told me you're on top of your 50 meter. That's amazing."

"Yeah. It felt good."

"Do you think…"

"Mom, what is it you used to tell me when Dad died? Baby steps."

"Okay, fair enough. But please start on your applications. You know our deal about your trip to LA."

"Yeah, yeah," I say, but in all honesty, I haven't thought about the trip in a while.

On my way out of the kitchen, I kiss the side of my mom's head. She seems a little surprised, but smiles genuinely.

I go up to my room and open my unfinished application. Only my name and address are filled out. Then I look at the laptop screen with the empty essay.

College seems like another world. Right now, I'm so focused on getting through each day. Waiting for the names to stop, or for me to see another one. How can I possibly write a college essay that would explain this?

My FaceTime starts going off, and it's Jenna. I let it go unanswered. I don't want to hear about celebrities. Something else is going on in my life, something way more powerful than celebrity sightings. I have been chosen to make a difference.

8.

stay focused

I wake to the buzz of my phone.

It's Jenna. I can't keep avoiding her.

"Hey," I answer groggily.

"Rough night?" Jenna says.

"You could say that. There's a lot going on."

"T, what is it? You have to tell me. I'm your girl."

So I do. While going through my morning rituals, I tell her everything. Apparently, now I'm the type of person who can pee while talking to her best friend, but everything is up in the air at this point.

"So wait, is he your boyfriend now?"

"Seriously, Jenna? That's your first question? I told you

that names are appearing to me and they are connected to real people who are dying that same day!"

"Yeah, that part...are you sure about that?"

"Look, Jenna, I know it sounds batshit, but it's true. And the helping people part? It's great. Like, I have this power."

"Well, remember you can't be the hero every time."

"I know. I just stood there while a kid leapt off the Dupont Circle platform."

"I actually read about that online. Maybe seeing that is messing with your head."

"Jenna, you don't get it. Let's talk about something else...oh, you'll like this. I'm swimming again! Or at least letting Coach time me."

"T, that's amazing! Remember when you couldn't even get out of bed?"

"Don't remind me."

"Now you'll definitely impress the pool boy out here."

"I can't believe you're even staying somewhere with a pool boy."

"And the towels are heated!"

"Sounds decadent. How's your internship?"

"The work part is boring, but the play part is fun."

"Sounds about right."

"I wish you were here. I've met friends, but they're not

real friends, you know? They're like, 'OMG text me' and then they never respond. Ghosting is like, a sport in this city."

I think about Jenna, and how if she were a real friend, she wouldn't dismiss my whole story. She would trust me. Maybe she's not who I thought she was. But there's no way I can cancel the trip; she would be devastated.

"Well, I'm still planning on coming," I add feebly.

"I'm counting the days. And you need to tell me more about Edge! Seriously, he sounds like a super snack."

"I wouldn't put it that way, but yes, he's very cute. In a skinny sophomore kind of way. Actually, I meant to ask you...that person who does your hair, do you think she might lighten mine a little?"

"Girl, they can work wonders on anyone. I'll ping you the salon info."

"Is she a woman or a man?"

Jenna laughs. "They're transitioning. Just call them Rochelle."

I notice my reflection in the mirror as I walk past. I always thought my hair would look better lighter. My eyes are a light brown/hazel mix, and lighter hair would make them... what does Jenna say? *Pop.* It would make them pop more.

"Okay."

"And T, don't do anything stupid."

"In other words, do whatever you would do?"

"Wow. You really have changed. I like it."

"Stay away from the pool boy."

Jenna laughs. "I got my eyes on someone else. He's an actor."

"Of course he is."

There's a silence on the line. I can't tell her I feel chosen, and that there's a reason, I have to find out what it is.

"Anyway, call me soon?"

"Okay."

After breakfast, I go to the pool. The woman at the gate actually smiles at me, and she looks familiar, but I can't place it. It's like when she smiles she's a different person. I don't think I'd ever seen her smile before.

I stretch, then swim my usual mile. I don't see any names, but I feel as if at any moment one will appear. I don't want to live like this forever, but there's a certain thrill to it. I keep almost seeing names in the water, in the clouds, in the trees. Or maybe it's my mind wanting me to see more.

I find the salon that Jenna texted me. Rochelle isn't there, but a guy they call Loopy does my hair. I guess they call him that because of his curly hair, but I don't ask. I watch him, methodically layering the foil wipes, humming along with the hip-hop song that's playing. When he's finished, he spins my chair around toward the mirror. It's hard to hold back my pleasure. I feel like a little girl again, about to go to the pool or get ice cream. I text a selfie to Jenna, who replies with a hundred emojis and hearts.

I decide to surprise Edge and see if he notices my new look. But he doesn't answer my texts. Maybe he's still doing "damage control."

On my way home, I pass the coffee shop on Connecticut Avenue where my father and I used to hang out, where he would get a cappuccino for him and a hot chocolate for me, and we'd share a scone. He always gave me the last bite. As I stare into the window, a flyer for a rock show blows in the wind and gets caught on my leg. I stop, take a deep breath, and peel it off to look. The band is called Jelly, and it says the show is July fifteenth, with the date spelled the long way, except most of the letters are crossed out. I hold it closer.

J U L ~~Y~~ ~~F~~ I ~~F~~ ~~T~~ E ~~E~~ ~~N~~ ~~T~~ ~~H~~

The letters that aren't crossed out spell a name.

Julie.

I drop the flyer on the ground. Someone walking by picks it up for me, handing it back. When I meet the person's eye, a tremor ripples through my whole body. It's the ghost man.

I start running in the other direction. I'm sweating, my heart is beating too fast, and I feel my stomach drop. I don't look back.

I see a lobby for an apartment building and there's no one at the desk. It's freezing inside, but better than a hundred degrees outside. I sit on one of the brown bubble chairs and start texting Coach. But every text I start sounds weird, so I delete it. This goes on for several frantic moments until I type: Can you call me? and press send.

My phone rings almost immediately.

"Tegan, is everything okay?"

"Yes. How's Julie?"

"My dog? She's fine, why?"

"Does she seem tired, or is anything off?"

"Tegan, what's going on? Does this have something to do with what you were trying to tell me about?"

"Yes."

"You know I've been thinking about that. Maybe it's not healthy to look for signs everywhere..."

"Coach, do you think you could get Julie checked out?"

"I guess. She actually hasn't been to the vet in a while..."

"See!" The tremble comes back. The front desk person

returns and gives me a strange look. "Listen to me. You need to take her to the vet. Now. Do you hear me? Now."

"Tegan, calm down. You're freaking me out a little."

"Coach, please. Trust me. I have to go."

The front desk person is now in front of me. I hang up and say, "I was just leaving."

All the way home, I continue to sweat and don't even bother wiping myself. I try to think if there's a pattern to this, but it's all so different, so arbitrary. A young person, a homeless person, an old person, an animal. It all seems disconnected. And who is Ghost Man? It's really confusing me. Right now, I pray Coach does what I told him. There may still be time.

When I get home, my mother notices my hair.

"Wow, that color looks amazing," she says. "What's wrong? You look like you've seen a ghost."

"I have."

"What?"

"Nothing. I used your credit card, but I'll pay you back."

"It's fine, Tegan. I'm happy you're swimming, I'm happy you're out and about...except, you look frightened, like the other day when you knocked over Larry's coffee. I know something's going on, and I know you feel like you can't tell me things, but I'm your mother. I'm here to protect you."

She hugs me, and I try not to cry. There's no way she can protect me from what is going on. This is way bigger than us, I know. I take a deep breath, pull back, and look at her. "It's cool, Mom."

"Okay. We need your application sent in, and you're good to go to Cali!"

My mother saying *Cali* sounds wrong. She always tries to remain relevant, but misses the mark, and it makes me feel sorry for her. I'd wish she'd embrace where she is in life and not always try to act younger. Life is turning out to be one big contradiction.

Back in my room, I check my phone. Nothing from Edge. I sit in front of my laptop, the file for the first college essay prompt still open, the cursor blinking.

What makes you unique?

I start typing to get something on the screen.

What makes me unique is swimming. When I'm in the water, it feels like coming home. And I am really fast. But when my father died in a helicopter crash, everything changed. I felt suffocated, numb. I wasn't motivated to do anything. I was ready to crawl into a hole forever. Then something miraculous happened.

I became chosen.

I saw signs.

I saved a life.

I woke up.

That's enough for now. My thoughts don't necessarily make sense on paper.

I put on the *Moth* podcast to try to distract myself. It works until my phone buzzes. I jump across my bed for it, hoping it's Edge.

It's not Edge, it's Coach.

You're not going to believe this...

There's something going on with Julie's heart.

The vet is keeping her overnight.

I feel the tremble once more, and tears burn the back of my eyes.

I text back with shaky fingers.

She'll be fine.

But the truth is, I don't know. Do we ever know if any of us are going to be fine? I don't think *she'll be fine* should even be an expression. But in this case, I have to believe I was able to help Julie and Coach. And that is real power. Like I feel in the pool. As if I could do anything.

I mark another *X* on the wall and check under my pillow. It's there, one of my father's medals that I always liked because it had a purple ribbon on it. I hold it to my chest and think of how he always made me feel safe. That as long as I was with him, the world was going to be all right. I think of the poem about the geese, and Jean Fordham's eyes, which were so distant but also beautiful, how her whole life had led up to that moment. Did she cherish every one of them? Were they all coming back to her in a flash? There are no words for the mix of emotions I'm feeling. I try to breathe deeper and relax.

"Am I doing what I'm supposed to?" I hear myself ask out loud. Then I put the medal back and turn out the light.

In my dream, my father is sitting at an old typewriter. He keeps pulling out the pages and handing them to me, but they're random letters and symbols, gibberish. I know I'm dreaming, so I stare at him. He's so handsome, so strong. There's so much light in his eyes. His expression is very serious, though. He's not smiling. He keeps handing me the pages, and I drop them on the floor, except there is no floor because we're floating in space. So the papers twist and fall like the broken wings of birds, until they disappear into the black nothingness.

Then I, too, am falling like the pages. I finally land on what looks like a big, orange beanbag. The papers scatter around me. Now they have actual words and letters that mean something. I get up to gather them and try to make sense of it.

9.

put yourself in unlikely situations

I run my finger over my father's army head shot that's been on the fridge forever. In the picture, he wears a crisp uniform, and he's smiling like a dork, but in a good way. During his two deployments, he saved a lot of wounded soldiers by evacuating them out of war zones. When I was a kid, I'd ask him about the people he had saved. He'd tell me details about them, like how they had curly red hair or a wizard tattoo. I remember being fascinated. I couldn't imagine ever being that brave. Yes, Jenna's dad was a doctor, but this was totally different—like, hero material. The worst part is that I never believed something could happen to my dad. I thought he was invincible. I was very, very wrong. And even though I do feel like this is happening for a reason, I know I'm not invincible, either.

After training at the pool, I decide to go to Edge's house. I haven't known him long, but I don't feel like he would ghost me, as Jenna said. He told me he lived below Toki Underground, the famous ramen place on H Street. It's borderline stalking, but what if something's really wrong?

The bus is filled with every kind of person. A gaggle of pretty Latinas in bright sundresses, a hippy-looking mom with a baby in a sling, some burly construction workers, and a nervous-looking skinny man with acne, looking at his shoes like they're the most interesting shoes in the world. Whenever I turn, I expect to see Ghost Man in the corner of my vision, but it's only regular people, for now.

When I get off the bus, I'm able to find the ramen place pretty quickly. What did people do before GPS?

There are rickety stairs leading down to what looks like a small basement apartment. I stand in front of the door for a few minutes before knocking. I would never have done something like this before, but everything has changed. Sometimes I don't recognize myself. My actions and words have a mind of their own.

Edge comes to the door, and he looks different. Smaller, tired...shy, if that's possible.

“What are you doing here?” he asks flatly.

“I was worried—you haven’t texted me back.”

“My phone decided to break. It’s not holding a charge. I asked my mom to get me another one, but it’s not exactly a priority for her.”

Behind him, in the small living room, I can see what must be his mother, unwrapping a Hershey’s kiss. She’s pretty, but there’s something sad in her eyes. Is he going to let me in?

“I’m so sorry. It’s just—while I was coming here, watching all the people on the bus, I was thinking about how their lives could end at any minute, and I had to do what my heart was telling me, and I knew you wouldn’t blow me off…”

Edge comes outside onto the landing and shuts the door behind him. He looks like he might scream or cry, or maybe kiss me.

“Look, Tegan, I really like you. But I’m not ready for you to come to my house. Do you like ramen?”

“Yes,” I say, even though I’ve only had it out of the packets.

He points upstairs.

“Order the red miso. I’ll be up in a little bit.”

“Okay.”

He kisses me on the cheek and hustles back inside.

Walking up the stairs, I feel a surge of relief. His phone broke. It wasn't me. He really likes me.

The ramen place is super hip. It has slatted-wood ceilings and colorful pictures of vintage Japanese cartoons are tacked on the corkboard walls. In one cartoon, two rosy-cheeked children with giant black eyes are involved in some kind of game with nunchucks.

The waitress is impressed that I know what to order without looking at the menu.

While waiting for my food, I check the times of some of the professional swimmers I follow on Instagram. I try to picture myself in that place. Qualifying for the Olympics, getting sponsored, having 50,000 followers. With everything that's happening, it doesn't seem so out of reach. I never liked the attention before, but why not? If I can make something of myself, I should, right?

My phone buzzes. It's coach.

She has a heart murmur

What?

It's fine, she just has to take medication now

vet said she got another chance

I close my eyes. The restaurant noise is a blur in my ears. Another chance. I gave Julie another chance. I text him back a thumbs up and a puppy face, along with prayer hands.

The waitress comes with my bowl and places it carefully in front of me with a smile. The steam rises and the smell is almost euphoric. Like a field of flowers in Vietnam, or what I imagine that to smell like.

"Don't be afraid to slurp," she says when she sees me hesitate with the chopsticks. "It's the custom in Japan. In fact, it's considered rude if you *don't* slurp."

"Good to know."

The dish is amazing, like a cacophony of flavors and textures. Pork, lemongrass, cilantro. I am immersed in the experience. I never thought I would have an appetite after my dad died. When my father was deployed, my mother and I would cook a lot, as a distraction, I guess. I'd put on a playlist of Lorde and Imagine Dragons, and we'd make lasagna or chicken potpie. She would pretend to sing the songs using a utensil as a microphone. I was young enough to laugh and not think she was dorky.

Edge comes in and sits next to me. He looks better, refreshed, his hair still wet from a shower.

"Are you gonna get some?"

"I'm good right now."

He seems a little nervous, like he's figuring out how to say something.

I take a spoon of broth and noodles and slurp it up.

"You learn fast," he says.

I smile, and he clears his throat.

"I hope you understand, it's not you..."

"I totally understand," I say, even though I don't really. Is it because he's poor? Is there's something he's not telling me?

"My mom's been pretty down. She's been making me watch old movies with her, and she's not eating unless I make something."

"You cook?"

"A few things. I love food, which everyone thinks is weird 'cause I'm skinny."

"Good metabolism."

"I guess. So, yeah, and the place is pretty dirty. But you can definitely come over sometime. Just to see, like, what the American dream looks like firsthand."

"Ha. I'm sure it's not that bad."

"Oh, it's that bad."

I take another bite and slurp, and as I put the spoon down, I feel it. Like a wave running over me. I look to my left and directly in front of me, under the cartoon on the wall, is one of those vintage name bracelets held up by two thumbtacks.

The name is *Gwendolyn.*

I almost choke on my noodles.

“Is it too spicy?” Edge asks when he sees my face.

I point to the bracelet.

“Another one?”

“I literally felt it before I saw it. And I think I know who it is.”

“Wait, you know someone named Gwendolyn?”

“Yes. She was…well, my nemesis on the swim team. She told me I had a big nose.”

Waiters and busboys move around us, but it’s like we’re in a bubble. *Gwen, really?*

“Well, we can’t let her die, can we? I think we should find out where she is, check it out. Are you finished?”

“Yes.”

I mimic writing something to the waitress, the international sign for requesting the check. I pay, we leave, and we make our way back to the bus toward Logan Circle.

“Where to?” Edge says.

“Well, Gwendolyn has always lived in the same house, about a mile from mine, on a really nice block in Georgetown.”

"Okay, then. That would be the place to start. And, I'm wondering: What else has she done that makes her your archnemesis?"

"Wow, where do I start?"

"I'm listening."

As we wait for the bus to arrive, I tell him about Gwendolyn, how for as long as I can remember, she's always looked down on me, never gave me the time of day. One time in fourth grade, she spilled cranberry juice on the seat of the bus before I sat down, so I had to walk around with a giant red stain on my butt the whole day. She laughed at my misery, she and her other blond, beautiful friends. And she cracked an egg in my purse in seventh grade, and it made me cry for days. The killer was when she kissed the boy she knew I was crushing on at the eighth-grade dance. At that point, I could have strangled her.

"Wow, sounds like a real charmer," Edge says.

The bus pulls up, and we climb on. Once we sit, Edge gets out his headphones.

"I'm not being antisocial; I just have to decompress when I leave my house. It will only take a song or two, and it will be even better with you next to me."

I'm okay with Edge and me not talking. Isn't that what normal couples do? Are we a normal couple? Is anyone actually normal? I look around. This time the bus is filled with a whole other crop of people. An ancient lady reading a Bible, some young Black kids horsing around, and a middle-aged couple arguing over a map. No Ghost Man, although I can feel his presence looming, as if he may appear at any moment.

A man in a uniform gets on, smiling as he walks past us. I wonder if he has a child, if one day he's not going to come home. I wonder what happens when people die. If they really disappear, or if they stay with us somehow. I'm starting to believe in the latter. I secretly wish for even an ounce of my father's bravery, his courage to get through whatever is happening to me.

I grab Edge's hand, and he squeezes mine. I can hear the beats from his headphones secondhand, like in the church when I first met him. They're faster than my heart, but both rhythms seem to work together.

10.

go with your gut

Gwendolyn's enormous house looks empty. There are no lights on, and all the blinds are closed.

"Maybe she's out of town…"

"Where does she usually hang out?" Edge asks.

"Oh, the rooftop pool at Vida Fitness. I always thought it was weird because she doesn't swim there, she sits by the pool like it's her accessory."

"It's not a bad accessory."

"Wait, you won't fall for the whole trust-fund Barbie thing, will you?"

"No. I prefer G.I. Janes."

I laugh, shutting out the thought of Edge being into Gwen. Then again, everyone's always been into Gwen.

But Edge isn't everyone. Not even close. I can't see it happening.

At the front desk of Vida Fitness, I convince the guy to let us up *to tell our friend something* (even though she's definitely not a friend). When the elevator opens, Edge grabs my arm.

"From what you told me about her...are you ready for this?"

"If I do nothing, it'll be like going down to her level."

"Hold on a second, now you're suddenly morally superior?"

"Edge! You know how this is messing with me. I'm trying to figure it all out, but my gut is telling me there's something here worth saving."

We walk over to one of the modular couches under a huge, white umbrella. The place is mostly filled with gay men, but sure enough, Gwendolyn and two other girls are gathered by the edge of the roof, taking group selfie after group selfie.

Edge groans.

I notice one of the girls has a giant water bottle with a red-colored liquid in it, and by the way they're passing it to each other and laughing, I'm guessing it's not cranberry juice.

"This music," Edge says, "it's unlistenable house." He

puts his headphones on as I continue to watch the girls. They're most likely laughing at someone else's expense, or at some tasteless joke. I get nauseous just thinking about it.

I look around the roof. Two guys are dancing in their tight bathing suits, and one of the pool attendants is shaking his head. A nervous-looking woman is texting on her phone, and she spills her iced tea. The attendant comes to her aid, and she swipes him away, not wanting his help.

The girls are still taking pictures, completely unashamed of their utter narcissism. Gwen is the one closest to the roof's edge. My heartbeat inches up to my throat. Is it going to happen right now? I stand.

Edge pulls one headphone off.

"They're getting buzzed," I tell him.

"Duh. Probably on Daddy's Grey Goose."

"She's getting close to the edge—what floor are we on?"

"Fourth."

Edge looks at them, but not like most boys look at them. He seems only mildly interested.

"So you really don't like rich girls?" I ask.

"No. Especially ones that were mean to you."

My smile is so big it might break my face. Edge has once again said the absolute right thing. I remember the day my father drove me to my eighth-grade dance. He was a chaperone, which would normally be totally embarrassing, but he was not that kind of father. I would never ask him to drop me off across the street, like I'd done with my mother. He always said the right thing.

I was wearing a white collared, button-down shirtdress from J.Crew. I was hoping Brian Mallory would ask me to dance. He had a girlfriend, but she lived in another town, and Jenna informed me that the girlfriend was on her way out and wouldn't be at the dance (she always knew the dirt on everyone). Dad parked, then turned to me and said, "Ready, pretty girl?"

I looked at the little mirror in the car's sun visor, and I was pleased. My lips were coated lightly with my favorite raspberry lip gloss, and there were two clips in my hair. "Yes," I said, flipping up the visor.

As we were walking in, he said, "Pretend I'm not here, okay? I'm not going to be hovering around you. I'm going to eat as many cookies as possible without seeming gluttonous." I smiled, knowing he'd only eat a couple. That was the difference between my mom and dad. He would indulge in sweets without feeling guilty. It was something we shared together. Secret ice cream trips.

The gym was decorated in shiny ribbons and a big homemade sign with a bad drawing of a wolf, our school's mascot. There was a DJ wearing a cheap black suit and a red tie. No one was dancing. The strobe lights flickered over a shiny but empty wood floor. Before we separated, my father gave me a slight nod. In that simple gesture, there was a lifetime of us knowing each other. The nod said, *Go, be you, you're great.* I walked over to where my friends were sitting in a circle under one of the basketball hoops. I joined the conversation, but the whole time, I was searching the periphery for Brian Mallory.

Finally, I saw him, standing with some friends, laughing. He looked completely hot in jeans and a sport coat. Eventually, everyone started dancing, but not in couples, more like clumps.

As I was debating approaching Brian, Gwen appeared next to me in a white silk dress that shimmered.

"I heard you have a thing for Brian Mallory," she said, like it was really cute to her.

"I guess." I never knew what to say around popular girls.

Then her voice got lower and she said, "Watch and learn," before strutting away. She walked directly up to Brian, said like, two words to him, and then led him by his arm into the corner where they proceeded to make out.

I was seething. I'm pretty sure smoke came out of my ears. Gwen could have had any boy at that dance, and she chose my crush? Why did she hate me so much? Because I beat her the year before at regionals in the 200 meter?

I walked over to my father to ask him if we could leave, even though I knew as a chaperone, he had to stay until the end. He said he'd take me home and come right back. When we were in the car, my father said, "The cookies were dry. But I still ate two. And did that DJ really play One Direction?"

I laughed. "Yes. It was all pretty sad."

"Well," he said, pulling into our driveway, "you were the prettiest girl there, and I'm not saying that 'cause you have spectacular genes on your father's side." I smiled, got out of the car, and went inside. In the kitchen, my mother started asking me question after question, but I tuned her out. Instead, I watched my father drive away, wishing he didn't have to go back.

Now, watching Gwendolyn, I can see nothing has changed about her. She is super pretty and does whatever she wants, but her smile isn't genuine. It's laced with malice. At that dance, I probably could have done the same thing with Brian Mallory. I didn't have the confidence. Yet.

As the three girls pack up to go, there's one who keeps dropping her sunglasses and laughing. She has a streak of blue in her hair, and a giant bird tattooed on the back of her neck. She doesn't seem to fit with Gwen's standard friends.

We follow them down to the street, taking the stairs after they get into the elevator.

Edge takes off his headphones and says, "Are we still going to save the Frosted Flake?"

"It's a *life*, Edge. Like Tom's."

I look at him, making sure he acknowledges that, and I'm thankful to see sympathy in his eyes.

"I know. I was only trying to be funny."

A little way down the block, the three girls approach a parked SUV, and the tipsy one with the tattoo gets into the driver's seat. Edge and I are pretty close to them. If I called Gwen's name, she would hear me. It hits me that she's about to make a choice. A really, really bad choice. And I could stop her, even though she's consistently made my life miserable. Edge is looking at me like, *do something!*

Just before Gwen closes the door, I yell, "Hey!"

She turns and looks at me, her eyes furrowed. "Tegan, what the hell are you doing?"

"Can I talk to you for a second?"

"We don't talk."

The three of them laugh like idiot canaries. I have half a mind to walk away, knowing the kind of person she is, but I know it's not an option.

"Please, just a second," I say.

"Oh my God. Hang on, girls."

She sighs and steps onto the curb with me, closing the car door.

"This better be good," she says. I can smell the alcohol on her breath.

"Oh, it's good," Edge adds from behind me.

"What the hell is going on here?" She starts to fix her hair a little, but is clumsy about it, and it kind of makes it worse.

"Gwen, listen. It's best you don't know all the details, but you can't get in that car. You have Uber, right?"

"Duh."

"Make up some excuse for leaving. Blame it on me. Your friend is too drunk to drive—who knows what will happen? Call an Uber."

"What are you, a freaking psychic?"

"Just do it," Edge says evenly.

She looks Edge up and down, then at me, like she's impressed that I'm hanging out with such a cute boy. It makes me happy, but it also makes me want to scream.

"You guys can't tell me what to do."

She turns to get in the car, and I know I have to do something more. It's as if my movements are involuntary now. I grab her Louis Vuitton bag off her shoulder and start running down the sidewalk, away from the car. My breathing is heavy. When I get to the end of the block, I stop and look back. Edge is standing on the sidewalk with her. It looks as if she's arguing with the girls, and they drive off in a huff. I walk back slowly to where they're standing.

"WTF!" Gwen yells, grabbing her bag back. "You are such a psycho."

"Gwen."

She's fuming, her eyes popping out of their sockets. Edge is getting a kick out of the whole thing.

"Get away from me!" Gwen yells, and the two of us back away slowly. Gwen is furiously tapping on her phone, obviously getting an Uber. When we turn the corner, Edge starts laughing.

"I didn't know you were such a good bag snatcher."

"There's a lot of things you don't know about me."

"Good. I like it that way," he says, and I'm not sure if I should be happy about that statement or not.

Edge looks at his phone for a minute, and then he leads me down to 17th Street where the Holy Crepes truck is parked.

"I saw this was here on Twitter. We need to distract ourselves with food. It goes with death. Or near death."

"Really?" Then I remembered all the casseroles my mom and I never ate after my dad died, all the fruit baskets and cheese baskets and loaves of fresh bread. "I never understood that correlation."

"It's about sustenance," he says, and his boyish expression makes me smile. I briefly forget about all the messed up stuff that's been happening. We stand in line at the truck, and he holds my hand.

"They're mostly savory," Edge says. "That's how crepes originated. Americans, of course, bastardized them and made them sweet. In France, they make only a couple of sweet ones, like Nutella, but today we are going with savory. My personal favorite is the ham and gruyère."

"Okay, let's get two of those."

We sit on a nearby stoop and eat our crepes, served on paper plates with plastic forks. I check under my crepe. No name.

It tastes so good, but I'm not sure if it's because of who I'm with—the sweet, funny boy who took me here.

"Takes a ham-and-cheese sandwich to another level, huh?"

I didn't even think I was hungry, but after the first bite I'm ravenous.

"Are you kidding me? Try another galaxy."

He smiles, knowing I said that because he likes other galaxies.

We eat in silence, watching people walk by. At first

I think one of them is the ghost man, but it's a skinny random with gray hair.

After a minute, Edge says, "What if her Uber gets hit by a bus?" I glare at him, then we both laugh.

"Seriously, though, should we have stopped the whole car?"

"How?"

"I don't know. Slashed a tire?" It doesn't sound like my voice.

"Wow. Breaking the law now. Do you like this playing God thing?"

"I wouldn't say *like*, but I do feel as if I'm some kind of, I don't know, vessel..."

"A vessel for goodness. Or maybe you're really clairvoyant."

As we head back to the Dupont Circle Metro station, he puts his earphones on my head and tells me to listen to the song. It's got a fast beat. I think about Gwen, how pissed she was. I wonder if the car is crashing as we speak. *Please*, I think, *let them live. I don't care if they're from the Gwen tribe. Everyone is significant.*

When we part, Edge kisses me a little longer than usual. Then he says, "You did the right thing."

"Hope so."

When I get home, my mother asks me how my day was.

"Okay," I say. "Edgar and I hung out. We got crepes."

"You really like this boy, don't you?"

I feel my face get hot. "Yes."

"Do I get to meet him?"

"Soon," I say, though I have no plans of them meeting. "He's busy a lot. His mom is needy."

"Ha! Do you consider me needy?"

"No."

There was a time, after Dad's first deployment, that my mother was pretty needy, but I understood. We hung out a lot together, because we both missed him so much. We'd go to the movies and sneak in food from home. We'd feed the pigeons in Thomas Circle, which I always did since I was a kid. But mostly, we would sit in the kitchen and talk. Me about swimming, her about her nonprofit and all the interesting people she worked with. She also turned me on to the *Moth* podcast, and we would listen to stories together, at dusk, the tree tapping the window. It helped us to temporarily escape from our own drama for a short while and go into someone else's world.

"Well, we were both needy for a while…"

Her look tells me she knows exactly the time I'm referring to. It feels like we're each pushing the wall between us, but it's too strong. The weight of his absence is too strong.

The news is on the small TV in the kitchen, and there's a picture of a car wrapped around a tree. My heart palpitates, until I realize it's not the same color as the tattooed girl's SUV.

"You okay, honey?" My mother is half reading a magazine.

"Yes, just tired."

"Okay. You know I love you."

"Yeah."

In my room, I collapse on my bed and my thoughts drift back to Gwen. I try to remember a time when she was actually nice to me. I can only recall one time, on an overnight field trip. Her parents didn't pack her a snack, and one of the chaperones asked me to share mine with her. I was reluctant, but she seemed very grateful. She was nice to me the next morning, too. But then she went back to being Gwen. Popular, rich, smart, bitchy, fastest swimmer on the team (besides me).

My mother checks in on me before she heads upstairs, and I tell her I'm fine, which I am. Just tired. Having second sight, or however Edge put it, is exhausting. I fall asleep easily, though, knowing I did what I could to help someone, even if that someone was Gwen.

....

The next day at the pool, after stretching, I sit on the diving board with my legs dangling over, waiting for Coach. There's barely anyone here, and the water is calm, but it's not exactly peaceful. In the corner of the patio there's a child's bike with one training wheel missing, abandoned and lying on its side. I hear a siren in the distance. It's hard to pinpoint why, but I can feel something is going to happen. The air is heavy, and so are my thoughts.

A few minutes later, a girl comes up to me, in tears. She's practically hyperventilating. It takes me a minute to realize it's Gwen. Her perfect façade has crumbled. Her face is all splotchy, and her hair's a mess.

She's trying to talk, but the words can't escape between her sobbing and catching her breath.

"Shhh. Calm down, it's okay," I say.

"No, it's not!" she yells that clearly. Some people in the pool turn their heads at us. I lead her a little farther away by the water fountain.

"I know it's not okay, but you're okay, right?"

"Morgan crashed the car!"

"Is she, are they…"

"No! Tegan, what the hell is going on? How did you know something was going to happen?"

"I had a feeling. Your friend was drunk."

She starts to quiet down a little, staring at me like I'm from another planet, like she's never known me at all.

"You had a feeling? This is completely insane."

She starts pacing and making exasperated noises.

"Just be glad you followed my advice. And let me give you one more piece. You should be kind to people."

She stops and stares at me, her eyes wide, as if she's registering what I've said in her brain. Her crying calms to a slight whimper.

"Are your friends okay?" I ask.

"Morgan's in the ICU..." She starts the heavy sobbing again, and I grab her hand.

"And the other one?"

"Harper is okay, only scratched."

I don't tell her she wouldn't have had the same fate. In spite of all the horrible things she's done and said to me, I hug her, right there beside the water fountain.

"Now that's something I didn't expect to see," Coach says, approaching with flippers and his giant parachute bag.

Gwendolyn nods to Coach, but then abruptly leaves, her body rigid and her head down. Coach doesn't pry; he knows that what happens between girls is between us girls. In fact, he looks a little intimidated, bless his heart.

"Okay," he says awkwardly, and leads me over to where we do our warm-ups.

Then, as a bunch of people gather around to watch, he straps me in.

The hardest thing in swim training is a parachute swim. You put a parachute on your back and swim laps. It's like you're dragging the weight of a house behind you. But when I do it, I'm more determined than I've ever been, and it makes me wonder how hard I could actually push myself.

If I can hug Gwendolyn, I can pull this parachute to kingdom come.

11.

do the best you can

My mother has asked me if I want her special smoothie a million times, so I finally take her up on it. And it actually tastes good. We sit in the kitchen, the early sun sifting through the tree branches outside our window, making gauzy patterns on the table. She starts to tell me what's in the smoothie, and I hold up my hand.

"I don't need to know all the ingredients."

"Okay, okay."

She's in her yoga clothes, her hair pulled up in a loose bun.

"I'm having dinner at the Jasons' later," she says. "It's been forever."

"Yes, it has."

My mother used to spend a lot of time with the Jasons. I

remember coming home from school to the three of them hanging out in the afternoons, thankful for the distraction. Instead of the usual peppered questions about my school day from my mother, the Jasons would entertain me. We'd make cookies and sneak bites of the batter, or they'd put on skits, pretending to be animals, or sing me songs about glamour girls with their "hair so high."

I never understood why they even liked my mother, but there is a part of her that I'll never know. The part that people from the outside see. My view of her will always be tainted by our mother-daughter dynamic. With my dad, I somehow got both sides. He was my father, but I saw him as other people did, too. That's what made his death even harder. Not only did I lose a father, I lost a friend, a hero, a partner in crime.

"Tell them I said hi."

"Will do. What are you doing today?"

Maybe try and save another life, I don't say.

"Probably hang out with Edge."

"Sounds good." Her eyes gloss over for a second, her face blank. I try to see what the Jasons see in her. The person and not just my mother.

"Can I ask you something?" I say, even though I don't have a question in mind yet.

"Of course. I'm all ears," she says.

"Don't say *all ears.*"

My mother makes a noise. "Why don't you write me a list of acceptable and unacceptable sayings?"

I smile and say, "Okay. It will start with Tee Tee."

"I've been good about that!"

"You're right, you have."

I take another sip of the tasty sludge a.k.a. smoothie. I look at the background picture on my mother's phone. It's a picture of Larry on a beach, wearing one of those wide-brimmed hats. I hold up the phone.

"What do you see in him? I mean, besides that he has money?"

She makes a face, but I think my question is reasonable.

"You'll find that even when the money's there, it's never about the money. Larry's easy to be around... He doesn't judge me."

"Did Dad judge you?"

"Look, Tee...Tegan, it's not right to compare the two. You and I both know they're totally different people. Your father didn't judge me, but I guess I judged myself more around him."

"Why?"

"Well, I always felt I had to be a better person for him.

He did so much for you, for our country, I always felt like I needed to do more. That's why I started the nonprofit. I have no regrets about that, but Larry is good for me, too."

"Dad wouldn't have liked him. Just saying."

We both smile at each other, and it feels like the first melted drop of an icicle.

"No, probably not. But it's important that we grow and change. I will always miss your father—you have to know that. I get that it was a hard transition for you with Larry coming into our lives, but give him a shot. He's okay."

She starts punching numbers into a calculator, looking through receipts from the renovation, which is about to start.

"New husband, new house," I say.

"New daughter, too, apparently," she says, winking.

"Still working on that one."

"You're doing fine. How are the applications going?"

"I started my essay."

"Great."

My mother gets a text, and I can see it's from her doctor's office. An appointment confirmation or something.

"Is that for a physical?"

A flash of fear washes over my mother's face, and I think, *please, don't ever let me see her name.* "Actually, I've been waiting to tell you until I knew more. They found a tumor near my ovary."

"What? Why didn't you tell me?"

"I didn't want to worry you…you've seemed uneasy enough lately."

She gets up and goes to the sink, rinsing out her glass.

"Mom…"

"It's fine. It's benign!"

I hear myself sigh, and keep breathing. If she only knew how close death is, how it's all around us.

"But they're going to remove it anyway. It's a minor surgery, totally procedural. And Tegan…" She walks up and touches my new hair. "I need you to be there. When they put me under anesthesia, and when I wake up. It only takes two hours. It's on Friday. Okay?"

"Of course, Mom."

"Promise?"

"Yes, promise."

She kisses me on the cheek.

"It's nothing to worry about."

"But your face, it looks worried."

"Well, it's a worrying thing, but really, I feel good about it. They're simply covering the bases by getting rid of it."

"How did you know?"

"I had some pain, and got it checked out. They gave me a CAT scan."

"Ugh."

"What?"

"Nothing, I just don't think I could handle anything happening to you, too."

"I'm great, Tegan. Honestly, I feel healthier than I've felt in a long time."

She hugs me and kisses my cheek.

"Okay, okay."

The doorbell rings, and Mom goes to answer it. The minute she leaves the room, I get that feeling again. That rush before it happens. My phone buzzes, and it startles me. I grab it from my pocket. It's a text from an unknown number. It says jonah lee. With shaking fingers, I text back, Who is this? Some typing bubbles come up like they're responding, but then the whole conversation disappears. *What?* My throat tightens and my heart picks up. My mother returns with her UPS package in her hand. I shove my phone back in my pocket.

"Honey, I know I've asked you this a lot lately, but is everything okay?"

No, I want to say. *Everything is definitely not okay.*

"I'm fine," I say feebly.

She seems to accept my answer, but isn't buying it fully.

"Okay, be careful. I'm here if you need me."

"I will."

When I get to my room, I try rebooting my phone. The text is still gone. But the name is seared into my brain, like the others were. If I could only find out who's behind this! I shake my phone and bang it against the wall a little, but nothing changes. I sit down and take a deep breath. And another.

I text Edge, whose phone has now been replaced.

Meet me at the Circle? Got another live one.

Okay be there soon.

Dupont Circle is scattered with the usual randoms, but also everyone else imaginable, because for late July, it's actually cool for DC. Suddenly, it feels like fall. Like new beginnings. My heart dips and swells when I see Edge come up from the Metro.

We hug, and he kisses me quick. There's no time for small talk.

"I googled the name," I tell him. "There was a few that came up in the middle of nowhere in Virginia, which I wouldn't be able to make it to in time. But the one I think it is…he's a skydiving instructor. There's a picture of him on the website. He's done more than five hundred jumps."

"Not anymore," Edge says. "Where is it?"

"I called. His next jump is at 4 p.m. in Churchville, outside of Baltimore."

"You think we can make it?"

"With some luck, yes."

"Let's do it."

I grab his hand, and we head back down to the Metro. From there we go to Union Station and catch the Northeast Regional Amtrak with two minutes to spare. We settle in our seats as the train pulls away. I'm fidgety with nerves, and Edge must notice because he starts talking to distract me. He begins to tell me more about his family situation from over the past few days.

"My aunt came back with some dude she picked up at a casino in Virginia. This guy was, like, super strung out. He was looking around at things he could steal from our house, not that we have anything valuable. Anyway, they took off again to some other casino. I constantly try to tell my mother that her sister is draining her bank account, but she doesn't really care. I'm like, what about me? I have dreams and they aren't to work as a busboy at

Toki Underground. Although they have offered, and I'd get free ramen."

I laugh a little too loud. "Or you could start a church landscaping business."

"Yeah. Super big prospects."

"Well, tell me."

"What?" he asks, even though he heard my question.

"Your dreams."

He sighs. Outside the window, the industrial buildings turn to fields and estuaries. The train conductor checks our tickets.

"I want to be a DJ," Edge says. "But I need more equipment. I know college isn't really an option, but most DJs didn't go to college. It's not exactly a profession you need a college degree for."

"They don't have a DJ degree?"

He smiles, but then puts on his serious face.

"No, but there's an association I can become a part of. To try and get gigs and stuff."

"Cool."

"What about you? How's the swimming going?"

"Yesterday I did a parachute swim. Coach was shaking his head. It would literally be stupid of me not to compete at regionals. I'm swimming faster than when I was training every morning."

"So you are having a Wonder Woman moment."

"I guess."

"Are you gonna? Compete, I mean."

"I think I am. Do you think I should?"

"Yes! I'll dry you off."

I laugh. It was a random thing to say, but it's funny, and I kind of like the thought of it.

When we get to Baltimore, I get us an Uber. Larry installed the app on my phone for emergencies. I should have told him that I have an emergency almost every day at this point.

On the way out of the city, we speed by graffitied walls and kids skateboarding, rows and rows of low-income housing. There are lots of rusting, overturned kids' bicycles and scattered trash in measly front yards.

I tell Edge what happened with Gwen, her coming to the pool in a mess of tears, and he shakes his head. "How does remorse look on her?"

"She looked terrible, actually. She's totally freaked."

"I would be, too. She should be appreciative, though, like, clean your bathroom for life."

"Hey, what makes you think my bathroom needs cleaning?"

"If you're anything like all the other females in my life, then…"

"You mean your mom and your aunt?"

"Yes, and my five other girlfriends."

My stomach drops, but then I see his smirk. Why does love make you so gullible?

"Shut up. And my bathroom is clean."

"Let me be the judge of that," he says.

I try to picture him in my bathroom...and my bedroom. Does he wear boxers or briefs? Is he a light sleeper? Would our bodies nestle together like parts in a machine? What do they call it? Spooning?

"Well, you're welcome to use my bathroom anytime." *And my bed*, I don't add.

When we pull up to the tiny landing strip, there's a closed gate but it's not locked. I tell the driver to wait for us, and we get out. I manage to open the gate enough for us to shimmy in. There are a few small prop planes with the seats taken out, and some people wearing huge backpacks loading into one of them. There's a small booth set up, and an official-looking guy with a blue jacket that says American Skydiving Network. His name tag says Patrick.

Edge and I both start to speak at the same time, and Patrick holds up his hands. "Hold on, hold on."

"Jonah. Is he here?"

"Yes, he is. He's actually about to fly some folks up for a jump. How can I help you?"

The propeller starts on the plane closest to us.

"Wait, he's *flying* the plane?"

"Yes. He jumps tandem, but he's also a pilot."

We both start running toward the plane as the propellers speed up. Patrick yells at us, but we can't hear him 'cause we're both screaming, "Jonah! Jonah! Stop the plane!"

But we are too late. The plane gains momentum and takes off before we are even close.

We walk back, out of breath.

"Can you radio the plane?" I ask Patrick, and he looks at me like I've grown horns out of my head. This is a small-time operation, clearly. His booth is made of cardboard.

"Do you know Jonah?" Patrick asks.

"No," we both say in unison.

"Then can I ask why you were running after the plane screaming his name?"

"She had a premonition," Edge says.

"Well, would you like me to give him a message?"

"Tell him to be careful," I say, and Edge grabs my arm and leads me away.

We get back into the Uber and watch the plane. Three different tandems jump out and three parachutes release. It's beautiful, the moment the chutes collect the air and billow open. Like a gasp for breath, or the blooming of three flowers in slow motion. I can sense the weightlessness, even from the ground.

"Is one of them your friend?" our driver asks.

"It's complicated," I say, almost under my breath.

We watch the jumpers land in the field, one after another, each of the parachutes collapsing on the ground in an elegant rush. Then the plane curves around to starts its descent. The wings tilt and it looks as if the engine is sputtering. My whole body tenses. I look over at Edge, and his eyes are closed, as if he's praying.

The plane lands with a spark and slows miraculously.

"Wow, tough landing," our driver says.

"Could've been worse," Edge says. We wait until the pilot gets out. He high-fives the jumpers, and they all have some sort of celebratory drink.

"It's not happening here," I say, "Maybe we have the wrong Jonah. But we should follow him in case, right?"

"Yes, I think so."

Our Uber driver gives us a concerned look, but then makes a face like, *Oh well.*

After a few minutes, Jonah gets into a pickup truck, and we trail his car, a few hundred feet behind.

"What are we going to do?" Edge whispers.

"I don't know, but we have to go with it."

"Well, I can't say being with you isn't exciting."

As we head back into Baltimore proper. Jonah turns into what looks like a trailer park, dotted with prefab homes.

"Isn't exactly Beverly Hills," Edge says, and our driver laughs.

Jonah pulls his truck into the driveway of a small tract home.

"Park across the street," I say.

Jonah gets out and stands at the front door, taking what looks like a deep breath before he enters.

It's silent for a moment, but then we hear a crash, and another, like someone's throwing things.

"Wait here," I tell the driver, grabbing Edge's arm. "C'mon!"

We get out and creep up to the side windows so we can see in. There's a woman who looks sick with rage, spinning around, yelling at Jonah, her hair all frazzled. She's talking about pictures she found in Jonah's phone. Jonah is saying he can explain. She grabs the closest thing to throw at him, which is what looks like a ceramic vase. He ducks and it just misses his head.

He tells her to calm down, and she starts crying.

"We should get out of here," Edge says.

Jonah tries to hug her, and she pushes him away. She still seems angry and sad, but not filled with the same rage as before.

"You think he's going to be okay?"

"Yeah," Edge says. "Let's go."

We run back to our Uber.

"You guys stalking that guy?" our Uber driver asks as we drive away.

"We thought he was someone else," Edge says.

"Ah, well, where to now?"

"Train station," I say.

On the train ride back, we're stunned, frozen in our seats. If that wasn't the Jonah I was supposed to save, then what happened to the one I was? After a while, Edge wraps his arm around me. It feels good.

"What pictures do you think were on his phone?" Edge asks.

"I don't know, but that woman was unstable."

"Yeah, but I don't think she was capable of killing him."

"You're probably right. I only hope someone named Jonah in rural Virginia isn't dying right now."

"Yeah. What about the irony, though? The guy has one of the most dangerous jobs in the world, but his relationship with his wife seems more challenging."

I didn't think of it that way. He's right.

"So what's the takeaway?" I ask. "You never know when you're going to meet your end?"

"Or choose your women wisely."

"Is that something your dad told you?"

"Yeah. Speaking of, what about *your* dad? Did he…you know…have special powers like you?"

"Not that I know of."

"I'm wondering if, you know…"

"Me too."

When we get back on the Metro, we're the only ones in the car. The rumble and shake of the train feels satisfying, like it's finally settling after what was a very unsettling evening.

"I'm so glad I met you," I tell Edge. "Please know that. Regardless of whatever happens."

"You don't even know," he says, and we hold each other tight. Then we start kissing. It's not like one of us kisses the other. We meet halfway. It's completely mutual.

The world around us, even the sounds of the train, completely goes away. We enter the sweet, heady space that only two people who are connecting in a deep way can inhabit.

At the next stop, an old couple gets on, and I think to myself, *I hope you're doing what you want to do today. I hope you're making the best of every moment. This is what we have. The here and now. Do your best, even at your worst.*

I grab Edge's hand as the train bolts us through the dark tunnel. The walls outside our window pass by in a blurry mess, but my mind and my heart feel surprisingly clear.

12.

i got your back

One of my earliest memories is my father pushing me on the swing in our backyard, face flushed with his first beer of the night. He'd yell out the name of a state, and I'd have to yell out the capital before I swung back in order to get pushed again. I knew all the capitals by age three. When I got older, every Sunday we'd drive out to the rolling hills of Virginia and listen to old songs on the radio. It didn't matter how on-key we were, we'd sing along, windows down, the road twisting and turning along with our thoughts. In fourth grade, when everyone was singing silly kids' songs, I was singing Johnny Cash. I knew the songs came from a different place I didn't know about, some deep longing I couldn't really understand, but I saw it through my father. The way his head swayed and his eyes sometimes watered.

It was around fifth grade when we started our secret ice cream trips. We'd leave through the back door while mom was doing the dishes, saying we were going to *take a little walk.* I was still small enough for him to carry me on his back. I knew I was too old for that, but I didn't care. I could've ridden on his broad shoulders forever. Some nights when it was really late and he could see my light was still on, he'd come in with two bowls of vanilla swirl, and we'd eat them quietly together. Then he'd pull on both my ears and kiss my forehead twice. I always thought Mom never knew about the late-night deliveries, but one morning she said, "I heard a fairy in your room last night! I know it was a fairy because it couldn't have been spoons clinking against a bowl."

When I got a little older, he started taking me to movies. Some, like *Slumdog Millionaire* and *The Hangover*, we promised to keep a secret. We also watched documentaries, a few boring ones, but one that stuck with me was *Food, Inc.* It opened my eyes to how food production is run by a few multinational corporations, and how fast food changed the whole game of what we eat. Sometimes uncovering the truth is scary.

I remember the day my father was first deployed like it was yesterday. It was snowing big, wet flakes outside our kitchen window. I was old enough to know that where he was going was very dangerous. I watched him put on his uniform, button by button. When he came to hug me goodbye, he said, "Remember, I'm the only man that will love you forever."

The first time he came back, his spirit was diminished a little, as if someone had stepped on his soul. But we still drove on Sundays, sang in the car, snuck out for ice cream, and he still pulled on my ears and kissed my forehead twice.

When he was deployed the second time, I wasn't home to say goodbye. I remember being so mad at my mother for not getting me out of school. I threw some stuff. It wasn't pretty. I never saw him again.

I always held that against my mother. She robbed me of getting to see him one last time, of saying goodbye. But now, looking at my mother on her perch at the kitchen table, plans and receipts scattered around her, chewing almonds, the sun making a thin glow around her head, I literally and figuratively see her in a different light. Too often the ones we love are the ones we hurt the most.

"I'm sorry," I say, out of the blue.

"For what, honey?" she says, still focused on her papers.

"Everything," I tell her. "I'm going to train." I grab my swim bag.

She looks up and smiles at me. "I love you. And let me guess, then you're going to see Edge?"

"Yes."

"I still want to meet him, honey. Everyone likes to walk on the *edge* every once in a while. Oh, that came out wrong."

"See? I can't subject him to the mom jokes."

"What if I sit there and nod and don't say anything?"

She's amusing herself. She circles a number and gathers her papers, tucking her pencil into her ear.

"You can talk. Just be chill."

"I'll try. And Tegan?"

"What?"

"I'm proud of you."

She looks at me seriously, and for a second I wonder if, like the ice cream trips, she knows what's going on. There's no way. She has that maternal, all-knowing power, but she's in the dark on this one.

"For what?"

"You know, moving on."

"I don't like that expression."

"Okay, then I'm happy you're living your life."

"Well, we never know when it's going to end."

"What's that supposed to mean?"

"Nothing. Life is short, that's all."

"It sure is. I remember changing your diapers like it was yesterday. You had the stinkiest poop in the whole world."

"Now there's a topic you might not want to bring up with Edge."

"What, you mean I can't tell him you used to projectile poop?"

"Mom!"

She holds up her hands in surrender. "Okay, okay. Go out into the world, be free."

I nod and turn to leave. Within seconds, I'm out into the world, like she said. But free? That's still up in the air.

....

I get to the pool in a matter of minutes. The woman at the gate smiles at me again.

"Looking good on the laps lately," she says.

"Thanks. You know, I've seen you a million times but never got your name."

"Sharon Moss."

"Wait, have I heard that name before?"

"I used to compete, but never qualified for the Olympic team." She looks down as if slightly ashamed.

"But you won regionals a while back, right?"

"Once."

For years I'd seen this woman and thought nothing of her.

"I have a picture of you from the local paper in a scrap-book! You look different."

"Age will do that to you. Also, I got hit by a taxi, twice."

"What?"

"I kid you not. The world can be cruel," she says.

"Do you still swim?"

"Yeah. I teach lessons, too, in the off hours."

"Cool."

She gives me a look like it's actually not cool, more like sad. Then she says, "I've got a son. He's been swimming since he was a baby. He's only ten, but he's got promise."

"Promise is good."

"I heard your coach talking to your mother on the phone. He said you're killing the times."

"Kind of, I guess."

"There's no 'kind of, I guess.' Own it, girl. Or you could end up sitting here, like me."

"I will. I am, I mean. Anyway, nice to meet you."

I go to my lane, and it's calm and perfect. I do my stretches, pull on my cap and goggles, then start with a medium-tempo freestyle. But as I start thinking about everything—Edge, the pilot and his wife, the ghost man, Sharon Moss…I begin to move faster. The crash of my arms against the surface is gratifying, and my breathing becomes more efficient. My flip turns leave a swirl of bubbles that disappear like I wasn't even there. I don't stop for 100 meters, and when I finally do, I'm panting. My vision is slightly blurry, but when I peel off my goggles, my eyes focus sharply. A girl stands in the lane next to me. It's Gwen.

"Hey," she says. The only word to describe her face is humble, a word I would never have associated with her. I don't say anything, simply stare at her, until she says, "Can I train with you?"

"It's a free country," I say. And just like that, something shifts between us. Like forgiving her has given me the power.

We swim for the better part of an hour, using each other for pace, but not racing. It's what we used to do when we were on the team together, except it feels more adult now that we're doing it on our own. Coach won't believe it.

When we're drying off in the changing room, she stops and looks at me, tears welling in her sky-blue eyes.

"Morgan's okay," she says, "but it'll take a while for her to recover."

“I’m glad she’s okay,” I say, zipping up my bag.

As I’m leaving, she calls out my name. “You don’t have to be a bitch to me.”

“You mean like you were to me for years?”

She snorts.

“You know,” I tell her. “My father used to say, there’re three things you need to do in life. Be kind, be kind…”

“And be kind,” she finishes. “But it’s more complicated than that.”

“Not really.”

She starts playing with her hair and gives me a mean look in the mirror.

“Who was the girl?” I feel compelled to ask. “The one driving the car?”

“My cousin Harper, from Baltimore.”

“You should think about who you hang out with.”

“At least I have friends.”

“See? Here I thought you were changing.”

“Maybe I am,” she says, straightening the collar of my shirt.

I could never have imagined this moment happening, and because of that, I say, “Let’s train again. Friday. Same time.”

Her face lights up for a split second, like someone plugged in a lamp, then pulled the cord. She regains composure. “Sounds good.”

I call Jenna as I'm leaving the pool.

"She says I have no friends, so I'm calling you."

"Who? Gwen? What's her deal? I can't believe you're training with her!"

I try to tell her about the accident, more of what is going on, but Jenna seems not only physically three thousand miles away, but also mentally.

"Are you preoccupied?"

"Sorry, I'm at a breakfast thing for young women in Hollywood. Someone said Jennifer Lawrence was here, and she brought scones."

"Well, I can't really compete with that. I'll talk to you later."

"Okay. Bye!"

I hang up the phone and get on the bus toward H Street. I know I'm supposed to be excited to go to LA and visit Jenna, but it feels as if all she cares about are celebrities. She dismissed my whole story, probably because she's pissed I'm training with Gwen. The two of them don't have a great history. I know the pilot may have been the wrong guy, but the names are real. They're happening. I wonder how long this will continue. There has to be an end to it; it can't go on forever.

This time, the people on the bus look like wannabe

businessmen going on their first job interviews. I secretly wish them luck. They'll need it. We all do.

I close my eyes, remembering my father in the waves, the fingers of the sun behind his head, the frothy, white ocean crashing around him. Our laughter, how it carried with the sound of the gulls who flew in arcs above us. When I open my eyes, I stare out the window, watching all the people go about their day. Some are smiling, even in this heat. Some are sweating, impatient and angry. But Edge is right, all of them are dying. Though hopefully not today.

Someone sits next to me and I pivot my head. Recognition hits me like a foot in the stomach. The ghost man stares at me hard, his black eyes literally inches from mine. I jump up and get off at the stop we're at, even though it's not mine.

From the curb, I can see him watching me through the window. His face looks serene. As if he's accepted whatever fate he has been fighting. I duck behind a streetlight. After I catch my breath, I look back, and the seat he was sitting in is now empty. The bus pulls away.

13.

the people you need are right in front of you

It's raining today, and I don't mind, because it has cooled the temperature a little. Edge has come prepared, even though his umbrella is a little wonky. I'm thankful for the excuse to huddle together as we walk to get lunch. I watch the drops on the sidewalk as they splatter.

I tell him about having Sharon Moss's picture in my scrapbook but never making the connection that it was her at the pool.

"Sometimes you can't even see what's right in front of you, huh?" he says.

"I guess you have to look closer."

"Yeah."

"Like in the church, when I saw you from behind. I almost left, but something told me to see who you were."

"Are you happy you did?"

"Yes," I say, a little too quickly. I feel that familiar swell in my chest and a lightness in my head. I had my doubts about Edge, that maybe he was only hanging around because of the names, as a way to get over Tom. But we're together, and it feels like both of us don't need anything more than that.

Minutes later we arrive at what Edge calls the Great Wall of Food Trucks. There are even more at this location. The smells are intoxicating. People are lined up to order even in the rain.

"Today we're going to get Street Mex," Edge says. "The recipes go back four generations. It's the kind of burrito that will change your life."

"The changing is already happening."

"Okay, *enhance* your life, then."

"We'll go with that."

He smiles at me, and in spite of it all, I have this weird sense that everything is going to be okay. *Please don't let me see a name*, I think. *Or the ghost man. Not today.*

We sit on the root of one of the giant, droopy trees that line the park. Edge puts down his jacket for us to sit on, and he rigs the umbrella in the branches above us to create a kind of canopy. We eat in silence for a while, until he says, "Mind-blowing, right?"

"Pretty much. Total comfort food."

"Yes. And tradition."

I check the wrapper under my burrito, and so does Edge, and we both smile with our mouths full.

A little kid walks by eating ice cream, his father holding an umbrella over both of them.

"Did you have any traditions? With your dad?" I ask him.

"He'd let me play pinball in the bar while he drank beer with his friends."

"Oh."

"It was cool, though. I mean, it felt like I was cool enough to go with him. On the way to the bar, and on the way back, we'd talk."

"About what?"

"Spiders, wrestling, astronomy. He knew a little about a lot of things. But mostly we'd talk about women, whom he called 'broads.' I'd look forward to those talks. Of course, he'd tell me stuff I was way too young to hear."

"Like?"

"Things I wouldn't say in front of a nice young lady like yourself."

I laugh. "A broad?"

"I know, right? But, it's weird—I have this fantasy that I'm DJing at this huge venue, and my father's in the front row, looking up at me like, 'Wow.'"

"I'm beginning to think moments like that are actually possible. What about your mom? How's she doing?"

"She's better. But yeah…I wondered if you could help me with something."

"Of course," I say. *Anything,* I don't add.

He shows me a file on his phone, which is a past-due credit card statement.

"My aunt, she's on a gambling-and-booze binge at another resort in Virginia. I need to go there, and somehow confiscate my mother's credit card. As far as I know, it's the only means she has to rip off my mother. She's at around six thousand now, but the credit line is seventeen. I swear, I have to get that card back. My mother has enough money problems as it is. She won't cancel it even though I've tried to get her to."

"So, you want me to go to Virginia with you and steal back your mother's credit card from your aunt?"

"Basically."

"Considering what I've been up to lately, that seems like a regular Tuesday."

He laughs, and, even in the dim light, his eyes shine. How a person who has obviously had a really hard life can have that much warmth inside him is a mystery, although maybe that's what gives him the warmth. Someone like Gwen, who's always had everything handed to her, comes off as cold.

As I eat my last bite, Edge says, "You have your driver's license, right?"

"Yes."

"So we just need a car."

I think about it for a second.

"I could ask my stepdad."

"Really? I thought you hated him."

"He's annoying, but…"

"Okay. A car, and I've got money for gas. The thing is, we're going to have to do it at night. So we won't be back until super late."

"I can think of something."

The rain has stopped. We get up, and I toss my trash in the nearest bucket. Edge does the same but makes it a jump shot.

"Okay, I'll text you later this afternoon."

When we part, he kisses me, and we both taste like burritos, but it doesn't matter. He whispers, "Thank you," and I whisper back, "It's nothing."

As I walk to Larry's office, I can't stop smiling. Are we dating now? Does this mean we'll go further? I'm kind of anxious to go beyond kissing, because it's unexplored territory for me. I'm guessing it is for him, too.

Larry's office, which he only uses part time, is in a nondescript brick building, but inside it's super modern, with gleaming surfaces and abstract art. He's surprised to see me, and maybe a little nervous when he offers me water, soda, a snack.

"I had a life-changing burrito," I tell him. "I'm good."

"Well, next time bring me one. What's going on?"

I take a deep breath and sigh. "First off, I want to apologize, and it's not because I want something from you, but I do."

He laughs. People always laugh when I'm not joking. What's that about?

"I treated you like crap, and I shouldn't have."

"Listen, Tegan, it's a tricky situation. I get it."

"But still, it's not like you stole my mother away from my father. It's that you're totally different from him, which is okay. I'm starting to realize that being different, or putting yourself in different situations, is a good thing."

He looks at me, like maybe he's impressed with what he sees. "Okay, I accept your apology."

His phone beeps. He tells his secretary to hold his calls.

"Now, what can I do for you?"

I explain that we need a car tonight. I say it's important, but play down Edge's aunt's alcohol-slash-gambling problem. I tell him we need to bring her medication, which is plausible.

He agrees to let me borrow the Toyota truck he never got around to selling after he bought his Range Rover.

"But if your mom finds out, I'm toast."

"She won't. Oh my God, thank you so much! There's one more thing. We're going to be late. So you have to cover for me, maybe say you saw me asleep. When I get home, I can sneak in without you guys hearing. I've done it before."

He thinks about it for a second, then gives me a conspiratorial look and says, "Okay, but you have to text me every hour on the hour until you get home. I'll keep my phone on vibrate."

Maybe it's his way of trying to bond with me more, but I'll take it. He pulls out his card with his cell number on it, slides the key to the truck off his key ring, and puts them both in my hand.

"It's parked on T Street by Thirteenth."

I feel like I could hug him, but I stand and say, "You rock."

"I'll take it where I can get it," he says, giving me a somewhat slippery smile that I disregard.

When I get home, Edge and I plan our mission by text.

At dinner, my mother goes on and on about the tile guy, how he is so talented and sweet, and she wants us to have him and his husband over for dinner. Larry sneaks looks at his stocks on his phone. I can barely eat because of nerves. I want everything to go all right tonight, but I also know it could be risky.

After dinner, Larry winks at me as he and my mom head into the living room to watch a movie. I tell them I'm going to chill and work on my applications, but sneak out the back door quietly.

Edge is already waiting for me when I get to the truck.

It feels good to drive. In Rehoboth Beach, my father's cottage was down a long dirt road. As soon as we would get to the dirt part, I'd sit on his lap and he'd let me steer. It was the biggest rush, and not unlike what I'm feeling now, especially since my passenger is one of the cutest boys in DC.

When we get to the freeway, he reaches over and takes my hand. I check my rearview even though now's not a time for looking back. We've got a job ahead of us. A whole future, I hope.

"So your stepdad turned out to be cool, huh?"

"Yeah, I feel kind of bad for judging him."

"We all do that."

"Yeah, I guess. It's time to do less of that."

"Agreed."

Edge turns the radio dial. He settles on an urban station and a Rihanna song comes on. I can hear him humming along to it, and it makes me smile in the dark. Whatever is ahead of us is going to be better because we're together. I've never felt this way about a boy before, but I could definitely get used to it.

14.

take chances

The resort is fancy and sprawling, like its own little city nestled in a valley with mountains on either side. We pass the casino, which looks like a giant ski lodge. I follow signs to the main building, park the car, and then Edge and I look at each other. There's still that spark in his eyes, but I can tell he's also a little scared. I remember Coach telling me a little bit of fear is good. It keeps you on your toes.

"Okay, let's go."

We get out and start walking to the main entrance.

"I have a plan," Edge whispers to me. "Go with it."

The front desk is occupied by a man with a doughy face wearing a bow tie. Edge waves at him, and he comes over to us.

"I can't remember our room number or even the building, this place is crazy," Edge says, handing the clerk his ID. "It's under my mom's name, Brannon."

Mr. Bow Tie smiles and says, "It took me months to find my way around here." He doesn't even think twice, drawing us our route with a highlighter on a foldout map of the resort. As we leave, he winks at me. I'm not sure if he's onto us, or into me. Either one is slightly unsettling.

By the time we get to his aunt's room (or technically his mother's room, since she's paying for it), it's almost completely dark out. There's a maid in her uniform doing turndown service. We watch her enter the room next door to his aunt's through the rectangle of glass in the stairwell. Edge cracks the stairwell door a little. A toddler runs by and drops his bunny rabbit. He gives us a weird look and points at us.

"Shoo," Edge says, and the kid moves on. We're now holding back laughter.

"Shoo? He's not an insect!"

"Why is he up, and where are his parents?" Edge says.

The kid runs back into a nearby room, and a woman scolds him.

We wait, and all I can hear is our breathing. There's a charge to the air, as if anything could happen at any moment.

We are only a few feet from the door. Close enough that when the maid leaves, Edge is able to reach out and catch it right before it shuts. She enters another room, and Edge motions for me to follow him. When we get into the room next to his aunt's, we start giggling. The air is even more charged now. The guests could come back any minute.

"I can smell aftershave," Edge says. "So they probably just left."

"What are you, a detective now?"

"No, but I watch too much Netflix."

"Me too."

There's a self-help book on one of the bedside tables called *Men Are from Mars, Women Are from Venus.* I pick it up and show it to him.

"Do you think we're from different planets?"

"You say that like it's a bad thing."

There's a small chocolate on the pillow in the shape of a bird.

"Random," I say, but start peeling away the foil and take a bite. It's cheap and chalky.

"Hey! Leave everything as is."

I wrap it back up, but it doesn't look right—one wing is bitten off. I think about the fact that my fingerprints are already on everything.

"Edge, are you sure you can't ask your aunt for your mom's credit card back?"

"No way. She thinks she's entitled to it because she helped pay off my mother's student loans, like, eons ago. But she doesn't even realize how much she's spending. Way over what she was owed. It's an addiction."

"Like this?" I say, and start kissing him. I can't help it. It's like I'm the girl in the movie now, the one I'd always aspired to be but never thought it was even possible. The confident one. The one who sneaks into empty hotel rooms with a cute boy. I've literally been thinking about it all night, sneaking glances at his lips. We make our way to the bed and lie down facing each other. Our eyes barely blink.

"What's the plan now?" I ask.

"You haven't heard of the patio hop?"

I giggle. "No."

We both turn to lie on our backs, staring at the ceiling. There's some commotion in the hallway, someone talking loudly in Spanish. *This is it*, I think, *we are totally busted.* But then it's quiet again.

"Me, either. I made it up."

Edge pulls out his phone. He tells me he put his aunt's iPhone on his Find My Friends app without her knowing by stealing her phone and accepting his own request. There's a little pulsing blue dot in the next building over.

"Looks like she's in the casino. She's a day drinker and usually doesn't last that far into the night. It shouldn't be long."

I put my hand inside his shirt. His torso is rigid and smooth. I feel like I'm outside myself, floating above, watching my own life play out. We kiss again. Things start to escalate.

"Wait," Edge says, stopping. "I want to do this, but not here."

"You're right," I say, even though I can't help feeling a bit disappointed. "Should we wait on the patio?"

"Good idea."

We get up from the bed somewhat awkwardly, and head out the sliding doors. It's like ten degrees cooler here, and it feels so good compared to the heat of DC. We sit, crouched together under a blanket of blinking stars. Edge keeps checking his phone, and I watch his face light up from the screen each time.

I must have fallen asleep on Edge's shoulder, because he wakes me abruptly and says, "We're on."

"What?"

"She's coming." He points over to the next patio. I can

see she left her outside door open. "The plan is, I'm going to jump over now, and when she gets in, she'll most likely plop her purse down and go to the bathroom. That's my window of time to go get the credit card. I know she keeps it in her wallet."

"Is she alone?"

"Yes. I think so."

Something about how Edge has planned this all out and is completely calm makes me like him even more. I may even be in awe of him a little. It seems like the fear I saw in the car is gone, and now he's in survival mode. I want to kiss him again, but he's off, jumping from one patio to the other like a trained assassin.

Her blinds are open, and from where I am, I can make out the back of the hotel room door. I see a quick flash of her face when she enters. Bleached blond hair, blotchy cheeks, and too much eyeliner. She is what Jenna would call a "hot mess." But I'm not so sure about the hot part.

She disappears from view, probably into the bathroom. I hold my breath as Edge goes in, and don't let it out until he's done. He jumps back over the patio and grabs me. "Got it!" he says proudly. We run out of the neighboring hotel room and down the stairwell.

Then we cross over to the main building, walking slower

so we don't look suspicious. I text Larry that all is okay and he sends back a winking face emoji.

We get into the lobby again, and Edge says, "One more thing. Wait here."

There are large wooden columns in the lobby, and I stand behind one, close enough to hear what he's saying. This time it's another clerk, a girl with a tight ponytail and a thin smile.

"Hi there," Edge says. "We actually have to go home early because my mom's not feeling well. She gave me the credit card and said to check out or whatever." He hands the girl the credit card and his ID.

"No problem. We will have to charge you for tonight, however."

"Okay."

"I'll print out your receipt. I'm sorry to hear about your mother. I hope she gets better soon."

When we get back into the truck, he says, "Step on it, babe."

I smile, thinking, *Babe… I like the sound of that.*

....

On the drive home, I see a billboard for what looks like a family resort. There's an elderly couple holding young children, who are eating ice cream. I ask Edge if he has grandparents.

"My mom's dad is in Florida. That's where she's going eventually."

"Is he cool?"

"I used to get cards for my birthday, with cash inside, but they would say other things than 'Happy Birthday' on them. Like, 'It's a Girl' or 'Get Well Soon.'"

"That's kind of funny."

"That's my grandpa. Anyway, he's got this whole life down there, and we aren't really a part of it."

"Same as my grandparents on my father's side. They came to the funeral and then we never heard from them. My mom's mom is cool, though. She knits me stuff."

"What, like mittens?"

I laugh. "No, like, socks and sweaters."

"Do the sweaters have reindeer on them?"

"No, usually snowflakes."

"That's a little better."

"They're actually pretty cool."

As we get closer to the District, I fantasize about pulling over at one of the motels we keep passing. We could have our own room, for a whole night, not some stranger's hotel room. Besides getting my father back and getting to compete in the Olympics, that would be the next thing I would wish for.

When I pull up to Toki Underground, there's a line around the block. Edge turns to me and says, "I'm going to thank you in a big way for this."

"A kiss will do," I say. Our lips touch, and we go back into that elevated state. Lost in the moment. So much so that I'm startled by a security guard shining his flashlight into the truck. He tells me I can't park here.

After I turn off the car, Edge says, "I've got some extra lawns to mow, and I have to go with my mom to some winery she's writing about, so I may not be around as much for a bit."

There goes my dream of spending the night together. I try to make my face look like I'm not about to cry.

The guard yells, "Move it!"

"Tegan, you won't go breaking and entering without me, will you?" Edge asks with a small smile. But, for the first time, I see real vulnerability in his piercing eyes.

"Edge, it's not like I have ten other boys on speed dial. I'll wait."

"Okay, I'll text you."

"I'll try not to stare at my phone."

He smiles, touches my cheek, then gets out of the car.

Back in my neighborhood, I park the truck a few spaces away from where it was originally parked. It's midnight, but I can see the Jasons are still up, probably having a dinner party. I can hear music from their piano. I climb up their stoop where I can see in, but they can't see me. A woman, with her back to the window, is playing a silly song on the piano, something about a girl who was the whole world: *her chest was Brazil, her back was Bunker Hill...* The Jasons are beaming at her, and the voice sounds familiar. The song is clever and funny, even to me. When she finishes, the Jasons start clapping and yelling, "Bravo!" The woman stands and takes a bow. My mouth drops when I realize who it is. My mother.

I run across the street and up into our own house. Larry's in the kitchen, on his iPad this time, but still looking at stocks.

"You made it home! Good timing. Your mother's across the street."

"I know."

I hand him the keys.

"Did you accomplish your mission?"

"Yes. Thanks again. It means a lot."

He nods like it was nothing. But his face has the satisfaction of having helped someone else. I know that satisfaction. My face must look like that, too.

"Tell me something, since when does my mom play the piano?"

"She knows a couple of crowd-pleasers, why?"

"She's playing across the street."

"Ah, I came home a little early because, the gay-to-straight ratio was…"

"Nonexistent?"

He smiles. "Let's just say there're a lot of pink shirts and loafers."

"Ha." I know that Larry isn't homophobic. He couldn't be if he was with my mom, but I can see how it's not his scene.

"Maybe next time you can invite over a bunch of your friends and smoke cigars and like, I don't know, go hunting."

He laughs.

"I would settle for watching football."

"Baby steps," I say, heading up the stairs.

In my bed, in the dark, I can still hear my mother singing. Sure, she used to sing me lullabies as a kid, but I never knew she could play the piano like that, let alone entertain a room. For a moment, I got to see my mother the way the Jasons see her. And it gives me a great feeling. I don't know what it means exactly, but it feels great.

15.

keep me close

I wake up starving, throw on a T-shirt and my dad's boxer shorts—I know that seems creepy but it's not; I wore them before he died, too—and head down to the kitchen. As I'm eating cereal I check my phone. Nothing from Edge. Only a text from Jenna showing me a picture of the room I'll be staying in. I can't even think about the trip right now, but I know I should—it's right around the corner.

Even though I haven't seen a name in a while, it doesn't feel like this is over. It also would be nice to know what it all means.

After breakfast, I head to my room and start working on my college essay again.

What makes me unique is swimming. When I'm in the

water, it feels like coming home. And I am really fast. When my father died in a helicopter crash, everything changed. I felt suffocated, numb. I wasn't motivated to do anything. I wanted to crawl into a hole forever. Then, well, something miraculous happened.

I was chosen.

I saw signs.

I saved a life.

I woke up.

I met a boy.

I started to see things differently. People, too.

I know my father is with me, and that there are things I must do.

There's a knock at my door. I minimize the file and say, "Come in."

It's my mother. She's holding a small box.

"I kept this for you, and I think it's time you had it," she says, putting it on my bed.

"What is it?"

"Some things your father had saved."

She hugs me, and I welcome it. I even squeeze her back. She looks at me with tears in her eyes and says, "You're so extraordinary, Tegan, you know that? You're beautiful, you're smart, you're—"

"What's going on, Mom? You're not sick, are you? That tumor really is benign, right?"

"Yes! I just heard your father's and my song. I'm a little emotional."

"Oh."

"You're the only one left that connects me to him."

I think about how I've been pretty brave recently, like him. That I've gone out of my comfort zone, broadened my usual scope. That's something Dad loved to do.

She walks up to the *Xs* that cover almost the entire wall behind my bed. She runs her finger across the columns.

"I still feel him. Do you?" I ask.

"Absolutely," she says. "I still expect him to be standing here, right next to me. But I'll never feel him like the way you do, because you're an *actual* part of him."

"I know."

She turns, patting her eyes with the edge of her finger. "What I'm trying to say is, I'm so grateful for you."

"Thanks."

She sighs and heads toward the door.

"Mom?"

"Yes, honey?"

"You're doing everything you should be doing. You're living your life."

She smiles and says, "Right back at you."

I don't tell her not to say *right back at you*. When she's gone, I walk over to the box and open it slowly.

There's a stack of receipts, and at first I'm confused, but then I realize they're for ice cream. From our secret trips. He must have saved every one.

It seems like everything in the box has to do with me. My grade reports (mostly good), my school picture from second grade (short bangs, ouch). A magnet from the Thai restaurant he used to take me to outside the city (I always got the pad thai). My driving permit test results (satisfactory).

Under it all is a crayon drawing I made of my father in a helicopter with a giant sun behind it. I look at it for a second, one of my tears dropping onto the corner, blurring the edge of the sun. I walk over to my desk and tape it to my wall.

....

Sharon is there when I get to the pool. She looks different again. Is it her hair? It seems bigger, like she had a blowout or something.

"Hey," she says.

"Hi. How come you never said hi to me before?" I ask.

"I've been kind of antisocial since I split up with my husband. But that's all changing now."

She shows me her phone. It's a man's profile on a dating site. The guy in the suit looks pretty generic, like it may be a stock photo. Still, I tell her he's cute. Which he is, if you like that generic-guy-in-a-suit sort of thing.

"I'm so out of the loop," Sharon says. "I've never dated in my whole life. I married my high school sweetheart, who ended up taking off with some girl to India. India! He hates Indian food!"

"I'm so sorry."

"It's been more than a year. I should be over it. I think he thought I was going to be in the limelight with swimming. When that dream died, so did his passion for me. But now I think I'm finally ready. I'm going on a date. It feels good, you know?"

"Good for you."

I go through the turnstile.

"Swim well," she says.

"Thanks," I say. "Your hair looks good."

She smiles, touching it with her fingertips.

"Just a trim, but yeah. Yours, too. You got it colored?"

"A little. Thanks for noticing. My boyfriend didn't."

It feels great to say *boyfriend*, even though Edge and I haven't defined what we are. But he asked me to wait for him.

"I bet he knew something had changed but couldn't pinpoint it. Guys aren't as good with details. As if I would know. I've only been with one!"

"Well, not for long apparently."

"Exactly."

I wave, and she starts scrolling through her phone again as I head off. I can see the resemblance to the Sharon Moss in my scrapbook now. Edge was right; I wasn't looking close enough.

It's cloudy today, which makes the pool give off a dull sheen instead of its usual bright shimmer. Gwen is already in her lane when I get there. She looks better today. I tell to her to pace me and that we'll start with the 200-meter freestyle. The water feels cold at first, but I give in to it, and eventually I'm warm. I concentrate on the angles of my upper arms and the undulations of my torso, on how they work together. After a few laps, other thoughts distract my focus. I picture Edge's aunt when she realizes the credit card is gone. I remember the warm feel of my fingers on Edge's smooth chest. I think about my mother singing that song. That makes me smile underwater.

After training, we head to the locker room to change, and Gwen says, "So, is that guy you were with your BF?"

"I think so."

"He's cute."

I give her a look that says, *Stay away.*

She puts up her hands. "What? I was just asking!" Then her pretty little pout sinks back into a serious face, and she says, "You can come over if you want." I still haven't heard from Edge, my afternoon is free, and nothing is normal anymore, so I say yes.

Gwen's house, perched on a hill on a leafy, brick-laned street in Georgetown, is pretty much a mansion. The massive white door leads to an expansive foyer, which is, like, three times the size of my room. Everything inside is gleaming like it's a photograph of a house in a glossy magazine, not a real house. I start touching things to make sure they're real. The kitchen has what seems like miles of marble and shiny chrome. There's a bucket of apples, like a still life I once saw at my favorite museum, and I pick one up. It's an actual apple, but doesn't seem to be ripening. I put it back without Gwen seeing. The fridge has a see-through glass door that reveals perfect lines of slightly blurred Pellegrino bottles and LaCroix cans and other colorful drinks. Gwen grabs us two Snapples and says, "Follow me."

Her room is basically the entire third floor. The bedspread is white and puffy, and her window looks out onto a giant weeping willow with a tire swing hanging from it. My father made my swing with rope and plywood. This one looks like it grew out of the tree, as if it's been there since the beginning of time. A group of starlings flutter around a small birdhouse that was made to look like a mini rustic cabin.

"This is out of a picture book," I say.

She hands me my drink and pulls up some music on her phone, which comes through hidden speakers in the ceiling. It sounds like country.

"You like this stuff?"

"Just listen. It's cool."

I expect the song to be cheesy, but it's not. It's more like a sad ballad of a guy who's been wronged by a girl, and it's genuine. It reminds me of some of the songs my father and I listened to on our long drives.

"I like it," I say.

"Tegan, how the hell did you know something bad was going to happen that day?"

"I told you..."

"A sign. What, like, some *Stranger Things*–type shit?"

"Basically. Without the monsters."

"I keep thinking about it. I'm sorry I was such a bitch. I'm so glad you stole my purse to get my attention."

Wait a second, Gwen apologizing? Weird.

"You should paint your nails," she says, changing the subject.

"I'm terrible at it."

"Oh. I could do it for you."

"Gwen, it doesn't work like that. You don't flip a switch from being mean to me and then paint my nails like we're best friends."

"Why not?"

"Because I don't really know you. I mean, you seem nicer now, but would you be hanging out with me if I hadn't, you know…"

"I don't know. But I know I'm starting to reevaluate stuff."

"Like, not getting into cars with drunk girls?"

Gwen makes an *ouch* face. "That, and I don't know, trying to be more real."

"Good luck with that," I say, and she giggles.

"C'mon," she says, shaking a bottle of nail polish, "what have you got to lose?"

"Any dignity I have left."

"Shut up. Give me your right foot."

Tentatively, I take off my shoes and she starts to paint my toenails dark red. As she carefully applies the polish on my left big toe, I say, “So, is this the ‘real’ Gwen? A nice girl who listens to sad country songs?”

She makes a noise. “I’m a lot of things, I guess. Not really a nice girl.”

“No. Look, Gwen, your house is incredible and all, and thanks for having me over, but why am I here exactly?”

She stops painting and looks at me hard.

“I saw a pic of the car. The whole back of it was crushed. If I’d been in the back seat, I would’ve died. You saved my life. I don’t want to be best friends or anything; we’re just hanging out. Is that okay?”

“I guess.”

“You still haven’t told me how you knew.”

My phone rings. Blood rushes to my head, thinking it’s Edge, but it’s Jenna. I let it go to voice mail.

“I had a feeling.”

She shakes her head and starts on my other foot. The first one looks good. Professional. Another country song comes on, and it’s so bad it’s kind of good.

“Why were you always so mean to me and Jenna?” I ask.

“I wasn’t.”

“Come. On.”

"Well, I don't know." She pauses painting, and her face gets blotchy. "Maybe I knew you were better than me, and I was jealous."

The words hang in the room for a while as the song plays. After a minute, she starts painting my toenails again.

"I knew you could look pretty without makeup, swim faster, get better grades. And I used to see you with your father. I saw the way he loved you, and I always wanted that. My dad's always in Asia—that's where his clients are. I don't think we've ever even done anything together. Except he drove me to my driver's license test. Big whoop."

A text comes in from Jenna.

Girl, where are u?

I turn off my phone.

"What about your mother?"

Gwen looks at me like, *You really want to know?* As if no one asks her that.

"She's got a lot of issues. She's addicted to benzos and plastic surgery. She spends most of her time at our house down in Palm Beach. I was raised by my nanny. I loved her, but she left when I was twelve. It pretty much broke my heart. I've basically been on my own ever since. It's only me and Ivan, our live-in cook, who doesn't really speak English."

"Wow."

"Yeah. The fabulous life of Gwendolyn Murray."

"At least you're popular." I say to try and lighten the mood.

"That's 'cause everyone wants to party here. Freeloaders and bottom-feeders. Even when my mom's here, she doesn't really care. But that's over now. After the accident, or avoiding the accident, I feel different. I realize a lot of people were using me for my house, for booze, for whatever."

"So you're not going to have any more parties?"

"No. I'm rearranging my priorities."

"That sounds like guidance counselor rhetoric."

She laughs. "Probably, but it's true."

When she finishes, she blows on my toes, and it feels strangely intimate.

"I'm sorry about your father," she says, and I can tell she really means it.

"This is going to sound weird, but I feel closer to him than ever."

The song changes again, and this time it's a girl, singing about *the one that got away*. I think about Tom Elliot sailing through the air, the curl of his scarf behind him. What was he thinking in that last moment? Was he finally going to be free?

Gwen puts clear polish on my fingernails, and after, Ivan the cook makes us chicken Caesar salads. He's a tiny man with a mustache and a sweet smile who speaks in broken English. After he leaves, I decide to tell Gwen about the names and how hers was one of them.

"Tegan, you expect me to believe that?"

"Believe whatever you want. I never thought I'd believe in anything when my father died, but I'm realizing this might be the key. You have to want to get out of bed in the morning. Whatever it is, have *something* to believe in. If you don't believe, you don't live. There are a lot of nonbelievers out there, and they're alive but their souls are dead. They've given up."

"So, what do you do next?" Gwen asks, picking the anchovy off the top of her salad.

"If more names come, you mean?"

"Yeah."

"Well, I do what I've been doing. React, follow my instinct."

"Why aren't you scared?" she asks.

"I don't know," I reply. "Maybe I get it from my dad."

"Duh," she says.

After we're finished, Ivan clears our plates like we're in a restaurant. Then he serves us a scoop of blood orange sorbet with a superthin cookie sticking out of it. It's delicious, and I wish I could share it with Edge, who would probably know some cool fact about sorbet.

"Well, I could never have imagined this happening," I tell her.

"What?"

"Sitting here with you, in your house, eating sorbet after you've painted my nails."

"Me neither."

I look at her, and she's not smiling, but her eyes seem different. There's a glint of kindness in them. It seems like the person I saw from the outside wasn't the real her. This is starting to become a pattern. Now, if I could only figure out the pattern to the names. And why I'm seeing them.

That night, in my bed, I grab my father's purple medal and hold it to my chest. *Show me a sign. Help me figure this out.*

16.

keep your enemies close

In my dream, I am at Rehoboth Beach with my father. We are sailing in his Sunfish. The ocean is such a deep blue it could be ink, heavy and churning, stretching endlessly in all directions. When the wind blows, pieces of his hair fall off and drift away, but then it instantly grows back. He sails the boat right onto a deserted island, and we laugh at a seal sunning itself on the sand. We both pull off our life jackets and dive into the water. He lets me jump off his shoulders, and like a dolphin in slow motion, I make a slow, elegant arc through the air, leaving a tiny splash as I cut through the water. When I come up, he's already at the shore. He's writing something with a stick in the sand.

When I swim in, I can see what he's written.

jeremiah park

His face turns serious, and black clouds form above us. The next wave washes away the name, and I wake up. I look over at my windowsill, and I realize that like the name in the sand, Tom Elliot's name was also in the same lowercase writing as my father's. Could he be the one behind the names? Is that why I keep feeling his presence?

I google *Jeremiah Park,* but no one comes up locally. I wish I had Edge to help me, but he's still MIA, so I text Gwen.

Do you know anyone named Jeremiah Park?

Within minutes, she texts back.

No but there is a kid named Jeremiah who skates at the skate park

My heartbeat starts banging in triple-time. That must be who it is. Jeremiah. Every single instance has been linked. There's a reason I know Gwen now. My whole body starts pulsating. This is what it feels like to have special power.

I text back.

You want to pay it forward?

Omg is this your Wonder Woman thing?

Yes. Meet at the skate park in twenty?

I guess.

As I'm getting ready, I finally call Jenna back and put her on speaker.

"I thought I lost you," she says, her voice sleepy. I realize it must be super early on the West Coast.

"No, I'm fine. There's a lot going on. And I'm coming in a week, so we can totally catch up." I figure I can fill her in then, although I don't think she'll really believe me. She practically dismissed it when I brought it up before.

"I miss you tons."

I want to say it back, but I haven't had time to miss her. Also, I feel like we're both becoming different people. I'm starting to wonder if it's okay to have a friend for only part of your life.

"How's the actor guy?"

"Ugh...end scene, I'm afraid."

"Oh, too bad."

"It's all good. I'm concentrating on my career anyway."

That makes me roll my eyes because she doesn't have a career yet. But she will, someday. I'm sure of that.

"Okay. Well, I have to make myself pretty. Big day at the film offices. Casting!"

At least she didn't name-drop. We say goodbye, and I tell her I'll see her soon.

....

The skate park is in the grungy-but-hip neighborhood of Shaw, which was formerly crime-ridden, but now is dotted with cool cafés and stylish farm-to-table restaurants. When we get there, the gates aren't open yet, so we go to this little coffee shop that's on the bottom floor of a row house around the corner. Gwen gets us both iced mochas, and we sit in the sun-soaked chairs by the bay windows. The AC is blasting, so the warmth feels good.

"So," Gwen says, "are you gonna compete at regionals?"

"I think so. It's weird. I wanted nothing to do with competing, and now I can't see my life without it."

"Yeah, for me it's been the one solid thing I have, you know?"

"I do." Except I now know that nothing is really solid—you just have to try for the best.

A woman comes in with her service dog, who steps on Gwen's white sneaker. She makes an agitated noise, then gets a napkin and cold water and starts cleaning it.

"So, you really think J-Rod's gonna…you know."

"J-Rod?"

"That's his nickname. His real name is Jeremiah Rodman. His father is a famous race car driver, and he's always in his shadow, blah blah blah. So he skates, for fun. But everyone knows J-Rod's the best at the park. I used to watch him skate all the time. He can do mad flips and shit, like, everything. He told me he named one of his signature tricks after me. The G-Fly."

"So why didn't you get together?"

"We did, but then I started dating Carson Langley, mainly because he was writing my English essays."

"What?"

"Hey, don't judge."

"You mean like you constantly judge everyone?"

"I'm trying not to."

"Well, I might need you today."

She continues washing her sneaker, which still looks dirty. Then she sighs and gives up.

"I'm here, aren't I?"

"Yes."

"So what's going on with your emo-dude boyfriend?"

I feel my cheeks redden. "We're good."

"He's pretty sexy."

"I know." I give her another *hands-off* look.

We both giggle, and again, it's like I'm looking at my life from above. *Me, giggling with Gwendolyn in a pool of sunlight? Surely this is some kind of montage from a movie and not real life.*

"I'd keep him around," she says, winking.

"Trying to. What about you?"

"I finally dumped Carson. He's too smart, if that makes sense."

"It doesn't."

"You know, a little on the nerdy side. He's sweet, though."

"He must have been devastated."

"He'll survive. Plus, I'm planning to go to college somewhere far away, like Portland, Oregon."

"That sounds nice. I might take a gap year and try to make the Olympic team. If I get into a school, I think they'd understand." The words are kinetic, tumbling out of my mouth on their own momentum, but they sound real as I say them.

"You could, Tegan. You totally could."

"We should try it together."

"I'm not sure I'm cut out for the Olympics. I'd like to do regionals, though."

I text Coach under the table.

Yes on regionals. Yes on Olympic trials.

He texts back a wow face emoji and ten exclamation points.

I show it to Gwen.

"He's intense."

"In a good way," I say.

Coach texts back again.

You will be living in that pool—got it?

I text back a thumbs-up.

"If you really want to compete in Tokyo, he's the man who can take you there."

"And you?"

"You're faster, Tegan, everybody knows that."

"If you trained enough, you could get faster."

"But in the water, you're, like, a *ninja*."

I laugh, then take a sip of my drink and look at Gwen. I wonder how many people we meet in our lives start out as haters and become friends—if that's what we are now—and how many stay haters. Is that why enemies happen? Because deep down they're meant to be friends?

We walk down to the skate park and sit on the benches outside the gates. There's a giant cement U-shaped curve, and some kids are warming up with small tricks.

"J-Rod's not here," Gwen says, putting her blond locks up in an elaborate, but messy, bun. "But he'll come. He's here every day."

"Okay, so when he does get here, maybe you can convince him not to skate today?"

"Yeah, I'll be like…'My friend told me you're going to die, so don't skate, and look out for buses on the way home.'"

I push her shoulder a little.

"I don't know, work your magic."

"Are you saying my only talent is seducing degenerate boys?"

"You're good at arranging your hair, too."

Now she pushes *my* shoulder. Then a kid with tattoos and a dog chain around his neck pulls up on his bike with his skateboard sticking out of his backpack. Underneath the skateboard, in big exaggerated graffiti letters, it says: *J-Rod.*

"Hey."

"Hey," Gwen says, like I'm not even there.

They stare at each other, in some kind of bubble. I clear my throat.

"What are you doing here? You stopped coming a while ago."

"I came to find you, actually."

J-Rod's cheeks redden. Gwen adjusts her hair.

"Cool."

As the three of us walk toward the skate park entrance, I start to text Edge again, but don't want to seem desperate. Instead, I send a purple heart, a secret shout-out to my dad.

We get inside the park, where it's only skaters, and sit against the chain-link fence. J-Rod is getting ready to drop in. I'm starting to get that feeling. The time is coming.

"Do something!" I stage-whisper to Gwen.

"Hey, J-Rod. Come here."

He walks over. He's carrying his helmet and scratching his head. Some of the other skaters are whispering behind his back. I'm sure it's about Gwen and not me.

"Wait, let me see that," Gwen says, grabbing his helmet. She runs her hand over a long crack. "Oh my God, you are *not* going to believe this. I once met Michael Fassbender in Paris and he had a motorcycle helmet with him. He told me that if the helmet is cracked, it doesn't work, like, it doesn't do its job. It was a random fact, but of course I remember it because Michael Fassbender said it to me in Paris… Anyway, look! I think it's an omen. You shouldn't skate today."

"What? Because of some pussy actor you met?"

"No, because this helmet is useless! And Michael Fassbender is not a pussy."

Another kid with spiked, bleached hair comes over and throws his own helmet at J-Rod, who catches it and looks at it.

"Not sure it'll fit."

"Try it," I say.

He does, and it fits. I feel like I can breathe a little better now. Thank God Gwen knew about the crack-in-the-helmet theory. Still, she doesn't look that worried. Next to her, I'm sweating and breathing fast. I must look like a scared animal. Because whatever is happening, it's still coming.

My body tenses up as J-Rod drops into the curve and up the other side, doing a couple minor flips and turns. Each time I wince, thinking something's going to happen, and hoping if it does, the helmet will save him.

He takes a break and comes over to us again, and says to Gwen, "Remember the G-Fly?"

"Of course," Gwen says, apparently forgetting why we're even here.

"Maybe we should bail," I say. "Go get milkshakes?"

"Yeah, if we were like, ten," J-Rod says. "Okay, Gwen, this is for you."

As he drops in again, all the other skaters stop to watch him. He seems to be going way faster than before. When he gets to the end of the curve on the other side, he glides into the air, twisting back. But the skateboard flies in the other direction, so his body is suspended in a slow-motion dance. Then he starts waving his limbs frantically. I look away before hearing the terrible thud of his body hitting the cement. There's a collective gasp that reminds me of the Dupont Circle platform and the end of Tom Elliot's life. *Please don't let this one die, too.*

A bunch of kids run to crowd around Jeremiah. He's writhing and whining in the crook of the curve.

I hear someone yell, "Call 911!"

The tattoo guy tries to move him, and I say, "Stop! You're not supposed to move him!"

Gwen is pacing, and she's making a weird noise, like she's wheezing.

"You should have done something! You knew this would happen!" she snaps at me, hysterical.

"I tried!"

The sound of the ambulance startles us. The crowd around J-Rod disperses as the EMTs burst onto the scene. They are talking in first responder jargon, but I hear one of them say, "Blunt trauma to the head." They get Jeremiah on a stretcher, and he looks unconscious. We run after them and insist on riding in the ambulance, telling the guys I'm his sister and Gwen's his cousin. I'm not sure they buy it, but the handsome EMT gives Gwen a look, which thankfully she doesn't notice, and lets us on. It's like on TV, except way scarier. One EMT is asking him questions, like who's the president, and the other is hooking up fluids. J-Rod is not responding. His eyes are almost completely rolled into his head, like he's some kind of zombie.

"Ask him again!" Gwen says.

The EMT tells her she must be quiet. The next few seconds go by in a blur as they fidget with various instruments, and then there's a loud screech and crash. I feel the ambulance jerk as it gets sideswiped by another vehicle. The sound pierces my ears. Gwen and I are screaming as we spin around and around, until something stops us short, and I end up on top of J-Rod, his spooky eyes inches from mine.

The back door has flown open, and I can see grass.

"Are you okay?" I ask Gwen.

"It's my arm, but I'm fine." She's crying softly, holding it.

Both the EMTs were slammed against the wall of the ambulance and are barely conscious. I dial 911, realizing how screwed up it is that I'm dialing 911 from an ambulance. They put me on hold.

I look through the window. The driver is conscious, but there's blood on his forehead, and he seems to be talking gibberish. Through the back door, beyond the patch of grass, is a parking lot. I can see the George Washington University Hospital emergency entrance. It's about two blocks away. Some kind of primal energy kicks into gear, and I know what we have to do.

"Gwen, let's go." I hang up my phone. "It will be faster. We have to take him!"

His IV has been ripped out of his arm, but he's still strapped onto the gurney. The ambulance is on its side, so we manage to push J-Rod and the gurney upright onto the grass and into the parking lot. We start rolling him down the sidewalk toward the hospital entrance. All these wide-eyed people jump out of our way and let us pass. When we get to the automatic doors, there's a man standing inside. Pale face, twisted smile. It's the ghost man. "Get out of my way!" I yell. I don't have time to be scared of him.

We get J-Rod checked in, and he's hurried away before we know what's happening. The EMTs stagger in one by one right behind us with the assistance of people from the crowd that gathered. Nurses come to check our vitals, and then tell us to wait in the lobby for further instructions. We sit on a bench, and someone hands us a bag of pretzels.

"How's your arm?" I ask Gwen.

"Better. They gave me Advil. I can't believe we almost died in an ambulance. And the fact that you don't have a scratch on you is surreal."

"Nothing can be explained at this point."

Gwen takes a slow bite of pretzel, shaking her head. We're both in shock.

"I don't think I can hang around you," Gwen says. "You're a liability."

"Well, you helped me today. You helped J-Rod."

"I hope so."

Gwen sighs, swallows, and shakes her head. She looks really scared, and it's so out of character for her. Or is it?

Eventually, an Indian doctor comes out and gives us a gentle smile.

"You girls are very brave," he says.

"She is," Gwen says.

"You are, too," I say.

"We need to keep Jeremiah for a while. We should know more in an hour or so."

"Is he going to be okay?"

"Hard to tell at this point."

Gwen starts crying, and I feel hot tears burn my own eyes, too. Why am I getting this information if I can't do anything about it?

"Hang in there. We will keep you posted," the doctor says. "And we've contacted his parents."

We sit there, crying softly, and I think about all the names, all the choices, all the near misses and quick saves. How are they all connected? The disinfectant smell in the hospital starts getting into my head, and my stomach growls.

"Look, Gwen, I'm gonna go home for a bit. I don't feel very well."

"Okay."

"Will you text me?"

She nods, wiping at her eyes.

Outside, everyone is going about their days, seemingly oblivious to the drama unfolding so near them. When I get home, I go straight to my room. I stare again at the picture I drew in fourth grade on my wall. I run my fingers over it slowly.

"I'm trying," I say.

I collapse on my bed. I must have fallen asleep for a couple of hours, because when I wake, the sun is going down, and my room is washed in a muted orange glow. I realize my phone is dead, so I plug it in. A few minutes later, it starts dinging like crazy. There are seven texts from Gwen.

3:29 p.m.

Concussion, still not responding.

3:38 p.m.

Had to give statement to police guy

3:49 p.m.

His father's here and is kind of cute, just sayin

3:51 p.m.

They let me into his room—J-Rod woke up for a minute and said he always loved me—it was weird but also unbelievable

4:58 p.m.

He's conscious!!!!

4:59 p.m.

It was the helmet that saved him. Omg.

5:01 p.m.

I want to like, run down the halls and sing opera

5:11 p.m.

Where r u?

I text her back.

Fell asleep. That is great news. Don't hit on his father.

She texts back within seconds.

Can we talk about what happened today? Holy shit—they're taking him home now. His father has smiled at me twice.

Glad he is well enough to go home. Stop flirting.

G2G. Talk tomorrow.

Then, there's a knock on my door. It's Larry. He comes in and closes it gently, like we're still in on some big secret, and asks, "Are you good?"

Despite everything, I get flooded with a hopeful feeling. Like maybe things with Larry will be okay. He's trying. But he still needs to get out of my room.

"Yes. See you later?" I hint.

He turns to leave. "Of course, of course."

I sigh, lie down on my bed, and put on a podcast, but I can't concentrate on anything. I want to talk to Edge. I decide to text him.

thinking of you right now

I look at my screen for the little bubble that indicates he's typing back. The bubble starts, and I sit up, my heart thumping. But then it disappears.

17.

stay afloat

I meet Gwen at the same coffee shop we went to before going to the skate park. The rain outside the bay windows is loud, and we have to talk over the noise. The once sun-warmed chairs now have a damp, dusty smell.

Gwen sips her latte and blows a wisp of hair out of her eye.

I look at her, trying to see her as a friend. After what we went through yesterday, I feel like we are now.

She grabs her arm and winces a little.

"How is that doing" I ask.

"It flares up, and the Advil barely helps."

"You didn't say anything about me when they questioned you, right?"

"What, that you're a psychic? No, I don't think that would've gone over very well."

"Did you see the news?"

"Yeah, the guy who was driving the van that hit us was a priest. He wasn't drunk. He was texting."

"I know, crazy. Were the EMTs all right?"

"Yeah, they asked about you. I told them you didn't have a scratch. They couldn't believe it."

"I got lucky."

"So, is it still happening? Your premonitions?"

"Not since J-Rod. But they could happen again at any moment."

She takes another sip, shaking her head. I eat the top part of my muffin. It's a comfortable silence.

"I also wanted to say again that I'm sorry for the way I treated you and your friend Jenna. I really am. I was being ridiculous. Ignorant. Jealous. All of the above."

I look at her, and her face seems open and genuine.

"Apology accepted."

A little later, the rain dies down, and a hush descends.

"I'm going to check on J-Rod. Text me later?" Gwen asks.

"Sure."

I watch Gwen as she hoists her bag over her shoulder, her

hair swinging as she walks out. I was always jealous of her hair. The thing I can't believe is that she was jealous of me. One thing is for certain: No matter how much you think you know someone, you don't. Not completely, anyway.

....

Sharon is reading the newspaper at the front gate of the pool. She doesn't look up when I get there.

"Something important going on in the world?"

She says, "Oh, hi. Well, I went on a date, and it was terrible."

"Oh no!"

"He flossed his teeth at the table."

"Oh my God. That's gross."

"It gets worse. He told me that he doesn't like living things around him."

"What?" We both start laughing a little. "What does that even mean?"

"Like, he doesn't have plants in his house, or pets, because it keeps him up at night knowing things are crawling around."

"Wow."

"I left before the entrée. But today I got matched with

someone who looks totally normal." She shows me a picture on her phone of a handsome guy with a *Mad Men*–style haircut, wearing what looks like a cashmere sweater.

"A doctor, he claims," Sharon says.

"Impressive."

"Yeah, we've been chatting. I'm going to try again. I'm reading the health and technology section so I'll have something to say."

"Sharon, dating is not like homework. Be yourself."

I grab her phone and check out her profile pic. She's smiling, and her eyes are genuine, but also hiding something. Her user name is Freestyler. Her byline says: *Former swimmer. Single mom.*

"You might not want to lead with single mom."

"It's true, though," she says.

I scroll back to the other guy. His eyes are kind of the same. Hiding something. His user name is Regularguy! and his byline says Doctor. Just lookin'.

Something about omitting the *g* in *looking* doesn't sit with me right. Like a fake attempt to appear casual. And why does his username have an exclamation point on it? Is he saying, *Really! It's true! I'm a regular guy!*?

"I think he's a much better prospect than the creepy-crawly guy."

She smiles, taking her phone back. "What about you, are you on any dating sites?"

"Me, no. I met my boyfriend IRL."

It feels good to say *boyfriend* again. Even if he is dealing with family stuff, and who knows when he'll resurface.

"Cool. Well, your coach is here, IRL, and he seems anxious. You should go. In the meantime, I'm going back to my crash course in scientific small talk."

She ruffles my hair as I walk by, and I think of all the times I'd walked by and never spoke or barely looked at her. How many times do we pass people who we could potentially connect with, but never do because neither person initiates it? I should make more of those connections and deepen my web. There is so much out there, undiscovered.

"Bye, Sharon."

"Swim good!"

Coach gives me a running hug. I had texted him about the accident, and he was freaked out.

"What were you doing in an ambulance anyway?" he asks now.

"A friend fell at the skate park."

"Can you try and stay away from skate parks and ambulances from now on?"

I don't tell him that I don't think it's over, that I don't

really have control over my destiny right now. Another name could come; anything could happen. Instead, I start stretching.

Coach shows me his plan, all printed out and bound in a special notebook. On the front it says *Road to the Big O.* He smiles sheepishly when he shows it to me. Inside is my training schedule (four hours a day?), time goals for the 200 meter (two seconds faster?), and suggestions for my diet (high-protein). It's all a bit much to consider at once so I just get in the water.

During my first few laps I think of nothing but speed, concentrating on the rhythm. But halfway through my second lap, I have to stop. I feel like I'm inside the ambulance again, dizzy and spinning. Coach comes to the side of the pool, brow furrowed.

"Tegan?"

"It's cool, I just..." I start coughing a little. *They checked me out at the emergency room and said nothing was wrong, but what if they didn't look hard enough?* "I just need a break."

Coach brings me water, and we sit on the bench, him dry, me dripping.

I can see Sharon in the distance, slumped at the gate over her phone. What if I end up a community pool attendant, a single mom scrolling Tinder? There's something about that thought that makes me panic. If I actually do make the Big O and get some major endorsements, maybe I could build a foundation for kids, and buy Edge his much-needed DJ equipment. I could also take Mom and Larry on a trip.

"You okay?" Coach asks.

"Yes, I'm ready."

"You sure?"

I nod, shaking out my legs and arms.

Back in the water, I get into my groove again. As I thrust, pull, carve, and snake through the water, I let myself get taken by possibility. I'm so glad I'm not sitting around being sad. My father would never have wanted it that way. He would want me to swim and to help people, both of which are empowering, and both of which I'm doing. And eventually, I am going for the gold. It sounds weird to even think it. That the girl who was holed up in her room not even wanting to go outside is now thinking about competing in the Olympics. But that's the beauty of life. Things can change when you least expect it.

By the way Coach dances around after my 50 meter, I can tell I'm making good time. I take a break and try to catch my breath. Some old guys, who are sitting on the bench by the lifeguard, clap. I wave to them.

It's like everything that's happening to me has put

another battery in my heart, and I'm supercharged. It's the same way I felt wheeling J-Rod down the sidewalk on the gurney. The water feels like a necessity, like stepping into my own skin. It's a place I'm meant to be. It always has been, but even more so now. I start in on my second 200 meter, remembering when my father first taught me how to swim. We were on the beach in Rehoboth, and I was about five, I think. A bunch of us were all gathered on the sand near the dunes. My mother was drinking wine with the Jasons, and they were playing some adult game I didn't get. Something about choosing a celebrity to marry or kill.

I was staring at some birds, and my father snuck up behind me and picked me up. "Water time?"

I had been waiting for him to ask me that. I sprang and jumped from his arms into the sand and ran to the shoreline, letting the foamy waves kiss my ankles.

He picked me up again and took me deep enough so only his head was above water. I clung to him tighter, my legs wrapped around his torso.

"Okay," he said. "Now when I let you go, you're going to move your arms and legs to stay afloat, and swim to the beach. Think of yourself as always above the water. Keep the water beneath you."

I resisted, saying *No, Daddy, no, Daddy*, and he said, "Okay, you can stay in my arms."

But after a minute, I got bored. Somehow, I knew I could do it.

"Okay, I'll try it. But will you follow me?"

"Every inch of the way," he said, his smile almost as bright as the sun glinting off the water in a million tiny pinpoints of flashing light.

He let me go, and I wanted so much to prove to him that I could do it. I tried so hard. A few times I almost went under, and I swallowed some water, cried a little, but eventually I made it, doing this deranged hybrid of the doggie paddle and the breaststroke. When I got to where I could stand, the sand felt like crystals of heaven beneath my toes. I lifted my arms up to the sun in victory. I swam in the ocean by myself!

When I got out of the water, they were all clapping, my mother and the Jasons. They were so happy. I was, too. I thought I would burst. Then my dad grabbed my wrists and spun me around. I felt dizzy and squealed with joy.

"Again?" he asked.

I nodded, and off we went.

Now, swimming a freestyle feels like it was programmed into my limbs. The water skims by me so fast I forget where

I am. There's only the bend and curl of my arms, the slap as they cut through the surface of the water, the sharp quick breaths, the coil and swish of release.

After training, we go to Coach's apartment to get Julie to take her to the dog park. Julie is so vibrant and so happy, we both stare at her in awe, knowing what we know. On the way to the park, Julie sniffs and trots and shakes her cute little head. At the dog park, she immediately gets in a tug-of-war fight with a golden retriever, and we sit in our usual spot.

I wait until Coach brings it up.

"Thank you for telling me about Julie, even though I'm not sure what I'm thanking you for exactly…"

"She seems to be doing great," I say.

"Yes. That was, well, that was either a sign beyond our comprehension, or a strange hunch."

"Coach, you yourself believe in stuff."

"Well, I'm definitely superstitious…"

"Yeah, this is like superstition on steroids."

"Wait, you're not on—"

"No!"

"That's career suicide; remember that."

"I know."

"So, do you feel like you still have, you know, powers?"

"Yes." I'm quiet for a moment. "I feel like something else is going to happen, something big."

"Whatever is going on with you, it's helping your times. You're killing it. So be careful—like I say with the water: Let it go through you. Keep your balance."

Julie finally gets tired of the tug of war and gallops back to us. She jumps onto the bench and nuzzles her snout in my ear, and it makes me giggle. But I stop when I see a man not so much walking as slithering by on the other side of the park. This time he has a blank look, but he's watching me as he passes. I quickly look away.

"Ghost Man."

"What?" Coach asks.

"Nothing."

Julie jumps up on Coach's lap, like she's declaring ownership. I realize that she's sitting here, right now, because of me. Coach smiles and scratches her ears. Then he gets serious.

"So, based on some emails, I've got three scouts coming to the regionals, one of whom is kind of a big deal, and they can recommend you for the Big O trials."

I give him a look.

"I know. It's what I call it."

"But you know there's another meaning, right?"

"I should hope so, Tegan. I was married for twenty years."

We laugh, and Julie jumps down, ready to put her leash back on. She knows it means she's going home for a treat. I check for the ghost man, but can't see him anywhere.

When Coach and I part ways, I call Gwen.

"Is your arm better?"

"It's okay."

"How's Morgan?"

"She's out of the hospital now. Also, we were on the news after the ambulance accident. The priest is in critical condition."

"I think we're meant to be alive at this point."

"Yes."

"I'm glad we are," I say. "But I feel like it's not over."

"How?"

"I don't know, I just do."

"Well, I hung out with J-Rod today, and I can't believe I never saw it all along…"

"What?"

"The way he sees me. He's so real, Tegan. He's not fronting. He doesn't care that I have money, he likes me for me, and I feel like I'm getting closer to who that is."

"I know what you mean."

"Look, be careful, and let me know if you need anything."

"Will do."

When I get home, there's a note on the counter.

T—

I'll be on my cell.

Remember my surgery is Friday.

Leftovers in fridge.

Mom

I go up to my bed and pull down the blinds, lying there in the dark. My phone buzzes, and it lights up the with a flash. It's Edge. Finally.

Miss you.

My heart expands like a balloon. Like when I'm swimming so fast that I'm hovering above the surface.

I start texting and deleting so frantically that my hand cramps. Then another text from him comes in.

Mom is better...winery is boring, though.

I start to text and delete as his third text comes.

I'll let you know when I get back. Any more names?

This time I can logically respond. I take a deep breath and type:

Yes but crisis averted, barely.

He texts back.

Good.

The next few minutes are brutal. The bubbles come up but then go away. We are both trying to say so much in, like, twenty characters. It's not working. Technology fail.

Finally, I give up and wait. A few minutes later, I hear the familiar buzz. And this time it's like a digital drug, making me light-headed and wanting more.

We fit

I stare at the screen for what seems like an hour but

is probably seconds. I try to think of what to type back. *Roger that*...no, that's something my mother would say. *I know*...too passive. I decide on responding with what's true, and type.

like puzzle pieces

18.

speak your truth

I'm standing at the edge of a pool that's in the center of a huge stadium that's filled with people. The sound is so loud I can't hear what Coach is telling me. I look up at the masses of people. I can hear them, but I can't really make out individuals—it's a huge blur. I bend over and stare at the expanse of blue before me, still and clean as glass. The gun goes off, and I'm startled awake.

I lie in my bed, staring at the *X*s on my wall. For a while, it was a way to make sense of my dad's death, to record the days he's been gone. But now it seems sad, and maybe a little self-indulgent. Today I don't write an *X*.

In the shower I think about Edge's text. A month ago I could never imagine texting a boy, never mind actually having a boyfriend. As I'm drying off, I look at myself in the mirror. I'm young. I'm pretty. I have a boyfriend. Maybe not officially, but it's kind of obvious.

But how long can this name thing go on? Surely not forever. I'd die of exhaustion. More importantly, will I find out why I was chosen? Is there enough evidence now to tell the authorities?

I dress and go to the kitchen for cereal. This time I eat the Cheerios with milk, and I'm hungry. I check the back of the box, but all is normal on that front. After I finish, I'm still hungry, so I whip up some eggs and spinach (part of Coach's meal plan). I check my phone while I'm eating to see if Edge texted back. He didn't, but there are several pictures from Jenna, holding up some frilly drink with a group of people who all look like they should be in a magazine. Before this all started, I worried about fitting into the whole LA scene, but it's last on my list right now. Even though the trip is only two days away, I'm kind of dreading it.

I clean my dishes and dry my hands, then stare at my father's picture on the fridge. It's starting to make me feel less hollow and more proud. Is this what the school counselor was talking about, time healing things? It sounded like a bunch of crap when I first heard it, but now it's sinking in.

I reach down to take the last sip of my orange juice as Larry comes up behind me. I startle, my knee hitting the underside of the table. Then, suddenly, I can feel it. A trembling, like it's about to happen. I could feel something rough against my knee on the underside of the table. As Larry gets his coffee, I sneak a look underneath. There's a name scratched into the wood: *Sharon*.

My jaw unlocks and my mouth falls open. I gasp.

Oh my God!

Larry is oblivious, still diddling with the coffee machine. My mother appears in her terry cloth robe, sighing. She kisses Larry, and they both go about their rituals. I try my best to act normal, but my mother can see right through me. I'm breathing weird and can feel my hands start to shake. I don't know how much more I can take of this.

"What's wrong, honey?"

"Nothing," I say, my voice cracking a little.

"Are you training today?"

"Yes." I put my empty glass in the sink. "In fact, I'm late."

"Okay, see you at the hospital?"

The surgery. I completely forgot.

"Yeah, of course," I say.

In minutes, I'm outside, walking toward the pool. There are some joggers, and a few randoms, but mostly the sidewalk is clear. Along with my legs, my mind is racing. Sharon. She was going on a date tonight. Is it something to do with Regularguy!? But what if it's something else? In that article I saved, it mentioned she had heart surgery when she was a kid. Is her heart going to give out on her? What am I supposed to do?

When I get to the pool, it's the skinny kid at the gate, not Sharon. I ask him where Sharon is, and he shrugs.

"Well, do you have her number?"

"No."

"Oh my God. Can I look around the desk?"

He gives me a funny look. I don't care.

There's a little desk to the side of the gate. It has a small drawer. I open it, and there's a receipt from a hair salon. It's a start.

"Thanks for your help," I tell the kid, even though he did nothing to help me. *Kill them with kindness*, my father used to say.

With the help of the map on my phone, I get to the salon in five minutes. They're not open yet, so I go across the street to Starbucks. I get an iced tea to waste time and check my phone. There's a notification about my flight Sunday. I can't think about that now.

A random with dirty fingernails and a baseball hat tries

to talk to me, but I pretend I'm mute and stare at him. He gives up, and I text Edge.

Saw another

In two seconds, the bubble comes and the sight of it makes me light-headed.

Omg wish I could help be careful

I send him back a thumbs-up and head back to the salon. There's a middle-aged woman opening the place. She looks like she could've been a groupie for some eighties rock band. She smiles at me, and I think, *This is good. This can work.*

"Hi there. You have an appointment today?" she asks, wiping down the desk with a spray bottle and a rag.

"Actually, I'm trying to find a friend. She works at the pool where I swim."

She stops, inadvertently pointing the spray bottle at me, like she's about to shoot me. "Who?"

"Sharon Moss."

She looks at me and says, "Oh. You're not stalking her?"

"No! We're friends. She works at the pool where I train."

"Gotcha." She starts spraying and wiping again.

"Look, I know you can't give out information, but would do me a huge favor?"

She stops spraying and points the nozzle at me again. "I could, but then I'd have to kill you."

She's joking, and I laugh, not from her joke, but because it seems like the funniest thing she could have said, considering, even though she doesn't know why.

"Could you call her, and ask her to call me?"

The woman puts her cleaning products away in a cabinet and sits at the front desk. She starts scrolling on the computer.

"Sure," she says, and I close my eyes and take a deep breath. "You know what, I'll give you her number." She smiles, writing the number down on a yellow Post-it.

"Thank you so much. You're a lifesaver." *Literally*, I don't add.

I leave the salon and start walking toward Dupont Circle. I find a house with an open gate and sit on the stoop. I dial the number.

"Hello?"

"Sharon, it's me, Tegan, from the pool."

"Oh, hey. How did you get..."

"Oh, we go to the same salon," I lie. "I was wondering, do you have a shift at the pool today?"

"Yeah, one to five. What's going on?"

I breathe a sigh of relief. "Nothing! I'll explain it later. At the pool. See you then. Take care of yourself."

I hang up and cross over 17th Street and walk down the alley. There are some randoms sitting against the side of the CVS. Their shadows are enlarged against the brick wall, like a gathering of giants. As I get closer, I can see one of them is the sailor. He still has his hat on. He looks sun-kissed and handsome, like if he put on a suit he could be at a dinner party. The line is that thin. As I pass, he smiles at me, his eyes open and clear. I smile back.

....

When I get to the pool, Sharon looks skeptical.

"Sharon, I need to tell you something."

"You sounded weird on the phone. And how did you get my number? The salon?"

"Yeah. But listen…" I try to think of a way to say it that doesn't make me sound like a street psychic. "I know stuff. Like, things come to me."

"What?"

"Tell me something. Are you going to this guy's house tonight?"

"Yes. Why?"

"You can't go to his house."

"We've been texting, and we spoke on the phone. Besides, I can take care of myself, thank you very much."

"Look, everyone knows you meet at a public place on a first date."

"Why are you so concerned? Are you a psychic or something?"

"Yes. No. I mean, it's complicated, you just have to trust me."

"Go swim, why don't you," she says, shaking her head.

I give up for now. I might have to stalk her after all. Unless she drops dead at the gate from heart failure. *Please let that not be the case.*

Gwen isn't here today. Her arm is still healing from the ambulance crash, but she's also been hanging out with J-Rod. It actually makes me smile. Maybe she needed to help save him to find out how much he meant to her. Maybe I needed to follow Tom Elliot so I could meet Edge. I'm beginning to believe everything is connected, even if it doesn't seem that way. It's overwhelming to think about, but also a little reassuring. We're on a conveyor belt of life, and there's no point in getting off; you have to keep going.

The water is all-encompassing. I start what is called my

maintenance training. A mile swim alternating breaststroke and freestyle. I'm astonished at Sharon's plan to go to a stranger's house. Does she not watch TV or read the news? It doesn't seem like she can be talked out of it. I don't know what I'm going to do, but I know I have to do something. That seems to be the only pattern here, which isn't a lot to go on.

In the changing room, Sharon comes in to pee. My mind immediately starts calculating. I rush out, knowing she probably left her phone on the little desk at the gate. It's there, and thankfully she doesn't have a password.

I go to their Tinder chat and find his address. 1201 Q Street. I wipe the phone with my shirt and put it back on the table exactly as it was. Then I take off.

I decide to get there first and scope it out. On my way, I get a text from Edge. It's a GIF of a chubby baby dancing. Underneath it says, This is how you make me feel.

Like a rock in a stream, I stop and look at it while pedestrians file around me. I text back eight hearts, but cut it down to three before sending.

Everything okay?

I think so. You?

I think so too—will fill u in

I send back a smiley face with a winking heart, then continue on my way. Regularguy!'s town house is the only one on the block that's been neglected. There are no flower boxes or fountains, only some trash bags and a broken chair. There's about three feet between his and the next house, but it's enough for me to scoot through. I see a window to the basement. It's fogged up, but slightly open. I pry it open a little further to peer in, holding my breath.

There are bookshelves filled with dolls; some are only bodies and some are only the heads. Their eyes are glass, their faces shiny. Some of the heads are thrown askew, like they've been chopped from their bodies. My stomach flips over onto itself and makes a noise. I adjust the window back to how it was and hurry out of the alley. There's an old woman standing there, holding a cat.

"Can I help you with something?"

"I'm scouting for a film," I say, remembering that Jenna mentioned that a few days ago.

The woman gives me a strange look, and the cat snarls.

"Sorry, I'm allergic," I say, and walk away.

A little way down the street, I stop and watch the neighbor woman go back inside, then I take a perch diagonally across from the house in question. The image of the basement is fresh in my head, like a scene in a psychological thriller. Why would he have all those creepy dolls? Something is off. Sharon cannot go in there alone.

My mother calls me, and I let it go to voicemail. Gwen texts me, and I don't respond. My head is fixed on the door across the street. Can I stop her outside somehow? Before I have a chance to answer that question, there she is, walking up the steps. Sharon doesn't seem fazed by the state of the house. A man answers the door in a suit and smiles, then lets her in. He looks both ways before he shuts the door.

I get a text from Larry.

We are at the hospital where r u?

Oh my God. The surgery! She's in recovery and can have visitors now. I completely blanked. If I leave, I could make it to the hospital in time, but if something happened to Sharon, I'd never forgive myself.

I start pacing outside his house on the sidewalk. What am I going to do? Should I crash their date?

I think about my mother, worried in her hospital gown. Then I see the name carved in the table. This is life or death. I have to do something.

I try to calm down, but what if he's already tied her up or something? I have to go with my gut. I walk up the steps and knock loudly on the door.

A curtain moves to the side, and I see a long, pale face. This time I actually scream. The ghost man.

The curtain falls back, and I'm back to pacing, my breath heavy, trying to get the courage to knock again. Two more texts come in from Larry of just question marks. "Ugh!" I yell. My mother is going to kill me. But if she really knew what was happening, she'd want me to help Sharon.

I knock again. Regularguy! comes to the door. He looks somewhat normal except his suit is a little too large, and his teeth are slightly gray. But when he smiles at me, it gives me the shivers. It looks like he wants to eat me for dinner.

"Hi, I'm Tegan, a friend of Sharon's?"

"Ah," he says, "I'm Geoffrey, with a *G*."

"A regular guy?"

He laughs, and it's almost cartoonlike, but in a flash, his face gets dead serious. "Would you like to come inside and join us for a drink? I was showing her my fish."

"Ah...what kind of fish?"

"Red-bellied piranhas."

"Wow. Well, could you maybe ask Sharon to come out here for a minute?"

"Why don't you ask her yourself?"

After all that's happened to me, going into this psycho's house, where apparently the ghost man lives, too, only seems mildly insane. My bar has been lowered considerably. *Sorry, Mom*, I think, *but I'm going for it.*

When we get inside, he locks the front door. With a key. What?

The place looks like an antique store, cluttered and stale-smelling. I follow him through what I'm guessing is the living room, and I almost trip over an old typewriter that's sitting on the floor beside the fireplace.

"My mother collected antiques," he says, leading me into the kitchen, which is surprisingly uncluttered. He opens the fridge and pulls out a pitcher of apple juice. "It's from the can, but I like it better this way because I can measure in a little more water. It can get very sweet, don't you think?"

"Um, where's Sharon?"

He laughs like he did at the door. That cartoonish bark. It startles me enough that I back up against the wall. He hands me the apple juice, as if I'm actually going to drink it.

"Sharon's in the ladies' room." When he says this, it is with complete decorum. Is this guy eccentric or is he a sociopath?

"So, is this a thing now, people crashing their friends' dates?"

"No, I mean, I'm so sorry. I needed to talk to her. It's urgent."

"She shouldn't be long now," he says, taking a small sip of the juice and clucking his tongue. On the counter, there's a bowl full of loose batteries and a bottle of what looks like woman's perfume. I flash back to Ghost Man behind the curtain.

"Do you live alone?"

Geoffrey stares at me blankly, and I can feel sweat forming on my hairline. "I prefer it that way. My mother left me this house. All her antiques. I might have a sale someday and move to Idaho or something." He laughs again, and I try to laugh along, like moving to Idaho is totally funny. Is Sharon tied up somewhere? Did he kill her already? He certainly seems capable. He is handsome if you look past the teeth, and certainly physically fit, but Sharon must get the sinister vibe that slithers out of him through his words, looks, and movements.

I hear a door open upstairs, but no one comes down.

I pretend to take a sip of the juice, and it stings my lip. How am I going to get us out of here?

Geoffrey is looking at me like he's planning how to skin me alive. I clutch my phone in my pocket. I put 911 on speed dial, just in case. He licks his lips and takes repeated sips.

I am starting to get really worried, when another door opens and this time, I hear shoes on the stairs. It's Sharon. When she comes into the kitchen and sees me, she looks embarrassed that her life has come to this. Dating creepy guys from the internet.

"Tegan, what...did you follow me here?"

"No, I saw you around the corner."

"Hmm," Geoffrey says, "likely story." He pours Sharon some juice, and as he's putting it back in the fridge, Sharon starts to drink it. I give her the hand across the throat sign. She rolls her eyes and puts it down.

Let's go, I mouth to her.

"Well, now that you're both here, why don't you come and see the fish? We can go from there."

So we go, the three of us, deeper into this weirdo's house. At least he's not showing us the dolls downstairs. I shudder to think what else is down there. The rotting corpse of his mother? It wouldn't surprise me. The back room is dark with red curtains, and there are gilded mirrors and ottomans that surround a large fish tank. Inside are two red piranhas, and one of them looks slightly deformed. I can see the serrated edges of their teeth. Geoffrey points as he tells us their names. "That one's Sodom and that one's Gomorrah." I notice one of his fingers ends at the knuckle.

"Hmm, that's not creepy at all," I say.

Geoffrey laughs, and even Sharon is looking desperate to leave now.

"Sit, sit. I have some treats to share."

We sit on one of the ottomans, and Geoffrey goes back to the kitchen.

"He has doll heads in his basement, and a ghost lives here," I whisper to her quickly.

"What?" she whispers back.

"We have to leave."

"Okay, let's go," she agrees. From the look on her face, I can tell she didn't need to be convinced.

"Wait! I'm still thinking of a plan. We can't just leave. He locked the front door from the inside."

"How did you see his basement?"

"From the outside."

"You really are a stalker."

"Shhh! Aren't you glad I came?"

"Yes. Sorry."

Geoffrey comes back into the room with a bowl of chocolate-covered raisins. I taste one, and they're definitely old, but they're not going to kill me. Sharon eats one, too, out of nervousness. Is this what internet dating is like for old people? No thanks.

Geoffrey starts talking about the mirrors, and how he has more in the basement. He talks about the rug, and how he has more in the basement. The third time he says basement, I stand and say, “Well, I should be going.”

“Me, too,” Sharon adds nervously.

“Whoa whoa whoa whoa, hold on, ladies, you just got here!” Geoffrey blocks the hallway.

“I’m not feeling so great,” Sharon says.

I start scanning the room for sharp objects. I see a framed college degree, with the name Rod Mallory. There’s also a picture of what I presume is his mother. She looks like a decent woman. Where did she go wrong?

“So, why don’t we all take a walk outside?” I offer.

“I’m not going to hold you against your will or anything, but I will ask you to perform one act before leaving. One that requires both of your cooperation.”

I try to remain calm. Sharon looks like she’s about to throw up.

“I would like you to kiss each other.”

Sharon stares at him, then at me.

“Listen, Rod,” I say, and his eyes widen.

“Don’t call me that.”

“Well, I’m not going to call you ‘Geoffrey with a *G*’ anymore.”

There's a back door to a small patio along the back wall, and a set of fire pokers right next to me. I know this is the moment that I have to do the right thing. A moment where if something goes wrong, it could go really, really wrong. I feel it. And lately, my intuitions are pretty spot on. So I do it. I slide the fire poker right out of its holder and in one swift motion, hold it up to Rod while motioning Sharon to the patio door. She starts crying.

"Go!"

She cries louder. Rod giggles, which is disconcerting, and says, "What are you going to do, poke me to death?"

"Sharon! Go!"

She runs out, still crying, and surprisingly, Rod stays where he is. But then he grabs the fire poker, and we struggle back and forth. We have the same amount of strength, so I'm able to hold my own. Until he lets go. I flail backward onto an old ratty couch. Then he's on top of me, the fire poker at my throat.

"Everything was going well until you showed up," he says softly.

My first instinct is to knee him in the crotch, which I do. He screams, and it's surprisingly high-pitched, and then he falls down in a heap on the floor. I jump over him and out the door. Sharon is climbing over the fence into the alley.

She's not crying anymore; she is running on pure adrenaline and in survival mode. So am I. We both get over it with little trouble. In the alley, we start running. We don't stop until we're almost a mile away. Then we sit on a stoop to catch our breath.

"Holy. Shit," Sharon says. "You were right."

"Did you not get the vibe that something was off when you walked in?"

"No, he seemed kind of normal!"

"Yeah. Goes to show, you never know."

"Well, I'm not going to anyone's house on a first date ever again, that's for sure."

"Maybe not a second, either," I add.

She starts tearing up again, except this time it's a quiet cry. "I kept thinking of my son, how if anything happened to me, he would be alone." After a pause, she adds, "But why were you there, really?"

"Sharon, I'll tell you, but not now. We need to get you home safe."

We walk in silence, the temperature dropping as we head deeper into the night. My phone has been buzzing with texts, but I haven't looked at any of them. My mother's probably getting out of surgery now. This is not going to go well.

At Sharon's house, she hugs me and says, "Thank you."

"You're welcome. I hope we never see Doctor Piranha Psycho ever again."

"I'm never going to get the image of that gruesome-looking fish out of my head."

"Do me a favor. Don't leave your house tonight?"

"Promise."

"Okay. See you tomorrow?"

"Another day," she says, shaking her head.

On my way home, I wonder if I should call the police and tell them I was assaulted. It could enrage the guy more, so I decide against it. But on second thought, how many girls don't say anything? Maybe a scare from the police would change him, prevent future victims? I call the anonymous tip line, saying I heard a man being physical with a girl at his address.

When I get home, the house is quiet. It's too late to go to the hospital, so I wait. When Larry and my mother come home, they don't look at me. My mother is weak, holding on to Larry for support. He sits her down at the table and starts fixing her tea.

"Did everything—"

"Your mother is fine," Larry interrupts.

Then my mother finally looks at me. There is so much emotion in her eyes: anger, hurt, amazement.

"I hope whatever you're doing is more important than your mother," she says, and it feels like her words are daggers going straight to the center of my heart.

"Mom, I would've been there, but—"

"But you're too wrapped up in your own world…" Larry is angry, but trying to hold it back.

"Not exactly," I tell them. "I need you guys to trust me. It was something important; it wasn't something stupid. I'm not being a kid. I'm being myself."

"Well, I thought I raised a girl who would show up for her own mother's surgery." She's crying now, and it makes me tear up as well.

"You did! Of course you did. Can you please trust me? I had to help someone."

Neither of them say anything. They simply sip their tea and shake their heads.

....

The next day, I feel the need to be with Mom and Larry, as opposed to avoiding them. Larry and I take turns doting on Mom, and none of us say much, but our actions are speaking louder than words can. We both love her, and she is grateful to have us, even if she's still giving me a bit of the silent treatment. She recovers quickly, and by the end of the day, she looks more like herself.

I tell my mom about training, about Edge, my applications, and what I'm packing for California. I usually despise my mother's incessant questions, but now that she's not asking them, I want to talk because it feels good to be with family—the family that I've got, at least. The people I know, who know me as Tegan, not some weird clairvoyant outlaw. And even though my mom doesn't respond much, I think my opening up to her makes her happy. Larry also listens intently, which is a quality I never used to see in him. But I'm looking at things differently.

That night I get another notification, this time to check in for my flight tomorrow evening. I check the weather in California and start to pack. I don't want to leave Edge, especially when I haven't even seen him in so long, and I don't particularly want to fill in Jenna with everything that has happened this summer, so the trip may be weird, but I have to go. A growing experience and all. Maybe it will be a good thing. Maybe.

19.

always remember

The next morning at the pool, Sharon hugs me again, really tight.

"I still can't thank you enough. You really saved me." She lets me go, then adds, "And are you going to tell me?"

"What?"

"How you knew."

"Look, Sharon, you like me, right?"

"Yes."

"If I tell you, your whole opinion of me is going to change, and I'd rather not risk it changing for the worse."

She gives me a pleading look.

"Just give me some time."

"Okay," she says. "But I've been meaning to ask, where's Gwen?"

"She was injured, and now she's boy crazy."

"Ah. Well, if you train with someone next to you, you will train harder. It's how it is. If you want me..."

"Really?"

"I could come an hour early on Tuesday and Thursday shifts. You know, when you get back from California."

"Sounds great."

As I walk over to my lane, I see Coach already there with the notebook. It seems like good timing, so I tell him about Sharon. "You know, she used to compete?"

"No."

"And she wants to train with me. On the days you or Gwen aren't here."

"That's fantastic."

"Listen, I'm going to stretch a bit, but can you talk to her, you know, get her up to speed on my training?"

"Up to speed, I like that." He considers for a second, then gives a *why not* face. "Sure, sure."

As I stretch, Coach approaches Sharon. She smiles at him right away. Their body language is stern at first, but both of them slowly loosen up, and I can hear them laugh about something one of them says. It looks like my idea is working. Coach's wife left him a few years ago, and as far as I know, it's been him and his pug. He's a little older than

Sharon, but they seem like a great match. Miles away from what the internet brought her last night.

I get in the water and adjust my cap and goggles. This will be my last swim before my trip, so I better make it good.

Coach comes back over, an ear-to-ear smile on his face.

“She’s great, right?” I say.

“Nice gal. I knew I’d seen her before; I didn’t make the connection.”

“That was my job.”

He smiles. “Anyway, I got her ‘up to speed’ as you said.”

“Maybe you could get her up to speed on some other stuff, too.”

Coach turns red, which I’ve never seen before.

“Okay,” he says, rubbing his hands together. “Let’s get started.”

During my first laps, my back starts hurting from falling so hard on that old couch last night, but I try and swim through it. I picture Sharon and Coach walking down a beach, sharing a bottle of wine, splashing each other in a hotel pool. Then I picture the same, but with me and Edge. We haven’t texted in what seems like a lifetime (but it’s really only been ten hours). Going to California will put us farther apart. Gwen told me the first guy you fall in love with won't last, but I'm bent on proving her wrong.

After training, Coach leaves first, and I wait as he lingers at the gate with Sharon. After he leaves, I gather my stuff and head to the changing room.

When I get to the gate, Sharon is trying not to smile.

"What did he say to you?"

"Nothing. He said I inspired him."

"You inspire me too!"

"Yeah, but I didn't make it as a professional swimmer."

"You can still inspire at many levels."

"No, you can inspire, Tegan. Not only are your fire-jabber skills top notch, but I've been watching you swim. And your coach knows his stuff. I wouldn't be surprised if you actually make the Olympic team."

"Well, for now I'm trying for regionals, not worrying about the bigger stuff. I mean, it's in my head as the end goal, but I'm focused on the present. You have to be to survive, right?"

"Right."

"So, did he ask you out?" I can't resist asking.

"Your coach? No!" She shakes her head, but I can tell she's actually pondering that idea.

"If he does, he likes jazz. And he has a cute pug named Julie."

"I love dogs. My son has always wanted one, too."

"Well, you never know..."

"Shhh. Don't jinx it."

....

When I get home, at my mother's billionth request, I work more on my college essay.

What makes me unique is swimming. When I'm in the water, it feels like coming home. And I am really fast. When my father died in a helicopter crash, everything changed. I felt suffocated, numb. I wasn't motivated to do anything. I was ready to crawl into a hole forever. Then something miraculous happened.

I became chosen.

I saw signs.

I saved a life.

I woke up.

I met a boy.

I started to see things differently. People, too.

I know my father is with me, and that there are things I must do. Like when you can sense something is different in a room, as if something has been moved, but you don't know what. I believe my father is speaking to me, even though I can't hear him. I know I'm supposed to do more than hide away. Even when he's not here, he's still teaching me.

It's been amazing to come out of hiding and change myself and the world around me. I'm training again, too, and I'm eventually going to try out for the Olympics. It seems incredible to think of how far I've come, from learning to swim with my father in the ocean as a five-year-old, to getting the best times in the 200 meter for our state.

But what really makes someone unique?

Being in the Olympics? Yes and no.

Getting good grades? Yes and no.

More so, I believe, it's being able to move on from hardships and be a better person. To learn the preciousness of life, to forgive, to open up your heart, to make the most of the time you have.

To eat life, not just taste it.

....

I go back to the box my mother gave me and look through the receipts again, picturing my father's face, the way he smiled, the way his strong arms felt around me. There's a fold in the bottom of the box where an envelope is sticking out. I didn't notice it before.

I pull it out, and a gasp escapes me when I see the lowercase handwriting on the outside of the envelope: *for tegan.*

I hold it in my hands like it's appeared from fairy dust. I hold it up to the light to make sure it's actually real. I shake my head a little. I'm not dreaming. I open it slowly.

dear tegan-

some thoughts and rules to live by, from your loving dad.

-i am with you

-there are no coincidences

-there will be ones that get away

-take chances

-find courage

-think of the possibilities

-give comfort

-be focused

-put yourself in unlikely situations

-go with your gut

-do the best you can

-i got your back

-the people you need are right in front of you

-take more chances

-keep me close

-keep your enemies close

-stay afloat

-speak your truth

-always remember

-fly

-reinvent

i love you

dad

Now I'm in full-blown sob mode. Like, barely breathing sobbing. My phone buzzes, and it's Jenna and Gwen checking in at the same time. Then my mother texts from upstairs, asking if I'm packed for my trip, but I ignore them all. I go into the bathroom and turn on the water. After I calm down a little, I read it again. There is a pattern there. It must be him. It has to be. The items on his list feel as if they align with the names and the experiences I've been having. I read it again, thinking of each one. The people who died and the people I saved and the people whose status is unknown.

Back in my room, I slide the letter under my mattress. My mother calls from the hall, asking if I'm ready. We're supposed to leave in twenty minutes. I tell her I am, but I'm not so sure. One of the last items on my father's list is *fly*. Does this have something to do with me getting on a plane? Or is it metaphorical?

I can't help it. I text Edge.

Found a letter from my dad...I think he's behind all of this.

No response, but I continue.

Does that sound weird?

Still nothing, so I change subjects.

How's your mom?

I start throwing things into my suitcase, trying to remember Jenna's texts about what to bring. Something about jeans, sandals, and crop tops. I don't have any crop tops, but I do have a few slightly more revealing T-shirts, which I include. Fifteen minutes go by, and absolutely nothing from Edge. I text him again.

Leaving on Delta from DCA at 6 p.m.

My mother calls from downstairs. I try one last text.

This is going to sound strange, but send me a sign.

You know, that you're all right.

I think of the letter, of Gwen and J-Rod, of the skydiver with the crazy wife, the old lady and the poems, the sailor and his tall tale, Julie the dog and her sweet face, Tom Elliot's pain I'll never know about. Sharon and how happy she seemed after talking to Coach. One of the Jasons used to always tell me that things happen for a reason. It always sounded like a big cliché, but I'm beginning to think he's right. You can't always make sense of the bad things, but you can try to trust that there's a balance to the world. It's important to be ambitious and proactive, but some things we have to let go, things that are beyond our control.

I have been through so much chaos, but I actually feel more grounded than ever.

I try to think of every memory of my father I have in my head: the beach, the boat, the ice cream, singing in the car, the movies, the park. There are so many, and they used to fill me with emptiness because they were experiences that we could never share again. But now they fill me with something bigger, warmer, brighter. Something like hope.

Before I leave for the airport, I tell my mom I'll meet her outside. I run down to the basement where the painters stashed the extra paint. I bring a can and brush up to my room and messily paint over all the *Xs* on my wall. I don't need to mark how long my dad's been gone, because the thing is, he never really left. He is with me and always will be. I have to be strong enough to carry him with me, and to believe. And to always, always remember.

20.

fly

On the curb, my mother kisses me at least ten times before I get into the UberBLACK car Larry ordered me. I know my mom is still mad at me, and frustrated that I couldn't tell her why I missed the surgery, but she's very emotional. In fact, both of them are acting as if I'm going to Antarctica forever.

"It's only California for a week," I tell them.

"Text me when you land, and call at least once a day, okay?" my mother says. Larry nods behind her.

"Okay."

The car smells super clean. My driver puts on reggae and starts bopping his head. It reminds me of the first day I met Edge in the church. I look at my phone once more.

Still nothing. Did his phone break again? Did something happen with his aunt?

There is a feeling of unease I always get at airports. I can feel it even as we pull up.

"Have a wonderful flight," my driver says. I like his choice of words. Most people would say *good flight* or *safe flight*.

I smile and thank him, then get out and head toward security. I have time, so I decide to stop for a smoothie. I drink it in the corner on one of the high, red plastic stools. The seat doesn't turn, which is mildly disappointing. When I was little, my father would spin me in the tire swing and then let it go. There was always that release, somewhere in the middle of becoming unspun, when I'd get fearful. It was the rush of teetering on the edge. It's kind of how I feel right now. I'm going to California. Does this mean the signs are finally going to be over? I can go back to being a regular teenager? Should I get an Uber back to my house and not go? Jenna would kill me.

Right as I'm about to enter security, I hear a voice behind me, real close.

"There she is."

I turn and find myself staring into those laser-green eyes I know so well. It's Edge, and he's carrying one of those miniature parachutes you get in cereal boxes. He hands it to me.

"In case anything happens, you know."

I hug him, and he smells just like I remember. Fresh-cut grass with a hint of citrus. I want to put him in my pocket, keep him there like a stone I can take out and hold on to for comfort. I could explode with happiness. I'm sure my face is super red.

"I was so worried about you," I say.

"I'm sorry. I feel like so much has happened in the last day or so; I haven't had time to do anything."

I want to throw away my boarding pass and grab his hand and run with him, outside, into the world, somewhere far, anywhere.

"It's cool. I only checked my phone, like, twice."

We both smile, knowing that's not the case. The security line is getting longer. A little kid starts crying.

"Listen, Tegan, there's something I need to tell you, and I needed it to be in person—I'm sorry I didn't text back recently."

"It's okay, but what? What is it? Your aunt?"

"Yeah, my aunt's in rehab. She no longer has any control of my mother's finances. I got a cop involved."

"Good for you."

"Thanks. But none of that's why I'm here..." He starts to pace a little, and it's completely adorable. Then he starts talking, using his hands to accentuate certain points. "Okay. I was thinking. The reason I like alien life and stuff, is because the one I've been given on Earth kinda sucks... that is, until I met you. And I thought I couldn't handle it, like you didn't fit into my world or me into yours or whatever. And now I realize that's the whole point. We *are* puzzle pieces, like you wrote. We're different shapes, but we work together. And no matter how imperfect my life is, it feels perfect when I'm with you. Ever since we met at the funeral of someone you didn't know. What are the chances of that?"

I try to rein in my tears, but they have their own force. They seem to be dropping at a rapid pace. Fast enough that my swiping can't keep up.

"I know," I say, hugging him again. Then he dabs at my cheeks with his sleeve.

I look down at the time on my phone.

"Edge, I'm boarding soon, I have to..."

"It's cool. Go to California, have fun, but know that I'll be here when you get back. Scars and all."

"Me, too. Scars and all."

We kiss, and everything around me becomes a bright, blinding light. We're standing at DCA airport outside of security, but it might as well be the center of the universe.

He waits till I get to the scanner that I have to walk through and hold up my arms. He blows me one last kiss.

On the other side of security, I go into a little bookstore and buy a paperback. It looks light and breezy, perfect for a plane ride to LA where I need to not think about how much I'm missing Edge. I get to the gate as they're boarding, remembering my dad's second to last item on the list: *fly*.

I get settled into 9A. The woman in 9B has brought her own food in small Tupperware containers and keeps smiling at me. Something about her eyes is unnerving. As if she knows something about me, or is planning something secretive.

I look out the window at workers in orange vests laughing at some joke. I check my phone. There are a bunch of texts. Jenna says, Safe flight! Gwen says, Be careful in Hollywood and come back soon. My mother says, Make sure you eat before your flight because they don't serve diddly-squat.

Don't say diddly-squat, I text back.

Adding to list! she texts back with a smiley face.

There's one more from Edge.

I wish I could go to sleep and wake up in 7 days

I text back.

I think that's the sweetest thing anyone's ever texted me.

And it is.

As the plane ascends into a mostly blue sky, I take out the paperback. Once again, I feel it before I see it, like a dark wave pushing through my chest and into my stomach. On the receipt, there are certain letters in bold, and put together, they spell a name.

Tegan.

21.

reinvent

I keep reminding myself to breathe.

I look around to see if there's anyone sketchy-looking on the plane. No one looks like a terrorist to me, but I have learned that people are not always how they appear on the outside. Everyone seems pretty normal, but you never know. Look at what happened last night.

I take two slow, deep breaths. Then another. And another.

Now that we're in the air and the plane has leveled, the face of the woman next to me has softened. Her eyes have turned kind. She gives me a conspiratorial smile and says, "Not used to flying?"

"Not really," I say, tucking the receipt into the seat back pocket.

It can't be me. I have so much to do. And my father would never let that happen. Keep breathing.

The seat belt sign dings off, and it makes me flinch. I close my eyes and images flutter, as if projected on the inside of my eyelids: my father's hands gripping the steering wheel, my mother collecting shells on the beach, the roaring crowd at my first regionals. Gwen blowing on my nails, Sharon blushing at the gate of the pool, Coach doing his dance. Then, the images turn darker. The ambulance spinning, the ghost man behind the curtain, the deranged piranha twitching in its tank.

I go to the tiny bathroom and lock the door, then stare at myself in the mirror. There are thin beads of sweat on my temples. I dab them with the cheap paper towel. Then I splash my face with cold water. I try to control my breathing. I look at myself, closer and closer. Something has changed.

Thousands of feet in the air, in a tiny locked bathroom, it comes to me in a bright moment, like clouds parting for the sun: Mine is the last name, so I have to die. The old me.

I'm a new person now. I'm wearing a second skin. It was a challenge, all of it. I can see that the ghost man is just death. He's not real. No one ever saw him except for me—he was a reminder. Death is everywhere, all around us.

It happens to everyone. Every day that you can live and not fear death is a good day.

And now my father is telling me it's okay, I can move on. So much has changed inside me since seeing that first name. Like layers of soil shifting under the earth, I have a new foundation. I'm swimming. I have a boyfriend. Gwen is my friend, and I'm able to see my parents as actual people. I know what it's like to forgive, to help others, to put myself in unlikely situations and not be so self-conscious all the time. And most importantly, I have learned not to be sad, because there are so many things to be happy about. My youth, my health, my swimming, my family, my friends… Edge. I miss him already.

My breathing has returned to normal as the last drops of water drift from my face into the sink.

"It's okay," I say to my reflection. "You're okay."

Back at my seat, I open my laptop and connect to the in-flight Wi-Fi.

I immediately start an I-message with Edge.

I saw my own name.

???

But I'm not scared!

??

I think it means I have to let my old self go.

The bubble with the dots comes and then disappears. The plane goes through a few bumps. The lady next to me smiles again, unfazed.

That makes sense, Edge writes, but I'm still going to track your flight.

I send a heart back, and he sends back two.

The lady next to me says, "Let me guess. You're messaging your boyfriend?"

"Yes," I say, completely and confidently, for the first time, and it feels amazing.

There's still a small part of me that is doubtful and scared, though. What if I'm wrong? Just in case, I draft an email to my mother.

Mom—

I'm sorry about missing your surgery. The thing is, I've been following signs. Dad sent them to me so I could help people. It was hard, and it was scary, but I had to take on the responsibility he left me. And I'm glad I did.

I know you knew about our secret ice cream trips. I know you lost a husband and a friend, and that his death was just as hard for you, if not harder. I'm sorry I shut you out. I know it wasn't your fault that I didn't get to say goodbye before Dad's second deployment. I can see you as the person you are, and I'm glad you're my mother.

Love,
Tegan

PS. Larry is cool, and I'm sorry for not being open enough to see that. I'm glad you guys found each other.

The woman next to me says, "Getting a lot done, huh?"

"Yeah, no distractions, I guess."

That seems to quiet her down. I hit send. Then I write another email. I'm on a roll.

Dear Coach—

Thanks for always believing me and pushing me harder

than I'd even thought I could go. You're one of the reasons I've started to believe I can achieve amazing things.

I think you know this, but swimming makes me feel the most alive. I can't believe I quit the team. That was the last thing I should have done. But sometimes we have to make wrong decisions to learn what was the right in the first place.

Don't worry, I'll keep training in California.

Hug Julie for me,

Tegan

I hit send. Then I realize, laughing a little to myself, that I should be writing these emails no matter what. It shouldn't be because I may not be around, because no one really knows how long anyone's going to be around. Why does it sometimes take death to appreciate life?

There is some more turbulence, and the seat belt sign comes on again. I close my eyes and make myself believe.

This is not my time. It can't be.

I look out the window and think about how much I have to look forward to, how my life is stretched out before me, vast and inviting like the endless clouds that look like an infinite duvet. After a little more turbulence, the plane settles. The pilot says we've gone through the rough patch and it's going to be *smooth sailing from now on*.

I smile, sinking back into my seat a little. In order to appreciate happiness, you have to know what it's like to be sad. In order to level off, you have to overcome the bumps. There will be more challenges ahead, but I feel stronger, better, faster. My heart is beating. For myself, for a boy, for life. Everything happened in order to teach me new lessons. I can see that now.

I decide to finish my college essay. I scrap what I was working on before and start from scratch.

What makes you unique?

I'm alive. I can see people for who they are, not just how they seem. I know that sounds advanced for someone who's a teenager, but trust me, the things that I've seen in the last few weeks make me feel like years went by. I've seen death, I've helped people avoid death, and I've stepped onto a new level in my life. I was given a chance to become empowered, and I took it. I'm still taking that chance now.

I know I still have a lot to learn, but I think I have some of the basics down. Mostly, I've learned that forgiveness can be a way to give yourself a gift. I guess a lot of seventeen-year-olds haven't been in the situation that I have, and that definitely makes me unique. I was challenged with some unusual tasks, and it forced me to change my reality, to overcome, to realize my own strength.

I'm going to try and compete in the Olympics in swimming, and I know that to achieve this kind of goal, I have to work hard at it. If something comes easy, it's probably not worth having. Someone told me that once, and it stuck with me.

I used to think that when my father died, a piece of me died as well, but now I realize that's not really what happened...

I stop typing and look out the window again. The sun is creating a thin, almost-neon line of red in the sky, tinting the fluffy clouds. The seat belt sign dings off again, and I lie my head back and close my eyes. I will work on my essay more, but it's a good start. Besides, when is anything ever finished?

We're all works in progress.

Epilogue

ONE MONTH LATER

There is not a single cloud in the sky, just a pure, brilliant blue. The sun is high, and the air has a hint of fall in it, a long-awaited release from the blinding heat of summer.

After hundreds of grueling hours training with Coach, I'm here. Regionals are about to start.

I'm in the tent next to the pool, doing my stretches with all the other girls. Some of them look nervous, some of them look calm. I'm somewhere in the middle.

I peek out of the slit in the tent. Coach is sitting next to Sharon in the bleachers, with binoculars around his neck. He's showing Sharon's son how they work as Sharon looks on with pride. He gives the boy the binoculars and then puts his arm around Sharon, who is beaming. A few days ago Sharon told me that Coach was the only person in the world who'll watch old swimming tapes with her. It made me smile.

Sitting above them is my mom and Larry. The renovation had them snippy with each other for a while, but they look pretty happy today. Larry and I binge-watched *Stranger Things* together, and I started drinking my mother's smoothies regularly. The Jasons came over the other night and told us they were getting married, and we all cried. Even Larry. We're happy for them. It feels like we're living in an important time in history. Equal rights and positive change are good things. Now I understand how one positive gesture can mean the world to someone.

Edge isn't here yet, but I know he's coming. After working hard on the application and submission process, he became a member of the ADJA (American DJ Association), and his first DJ gig was at a bat mitzvah. I crashed it without him knowing. He had the kids dancing to EDM and mixed in a few classic pop hits. He was glowing up there on that little stage. Afterward, we went to Rock Creek Park and made out in the bushes. Eventually, he let me into his house (his bedroom too).

Today is going to be great. I can feel it.

I stretch some more, then drink some green juice my mother packed in a cooler for me. I sneak another look up at the bleachers. Gwen has arrived, with J-Rod by her side. I watch Jenna walk up and sit on the other side of them. Gwen nods to her, but that's about it. If I'm going to be friends with both of them, I might have to compartmentalize a little. The truth is, all three of us have become different people, so who knows what will happen. Jenna and I have grown apart (California was fun, but not what either of us expected), but we'll always have our history. And Gwen's the person I always thought I'd hate forever, and now I'll always care about her forever. She couldn't compete because of her arm, but she wants to next year.

The crowd is starting to really fill up. We're minutes from the first 50 meter. I scan the bleachers one last time. My mother is laughing at something Larry said, and Coach is giving me his wiggly thumbs-up. Sharon and her son are hollering. And there, right behind everyone, is Edge, and his mother. Even from here, I can see he's telling her something. He looks proud. Proud that I'm his girl.

I wave to them. They all wave back.

Everyone's here. All the people I love. Except for one.

I walk onto my platform to shake out my arms and legs one last time.

This is my moment. And I am present. The pool is long and reflecting the perfect blue sky, waiting for me to carve through the water. I look at the time board, and for a second, the digital numbers seem to transform into letters, flashing a name: *Graham.*

My father's name.

The name isn't accompanied by that feeling I got with the others. Is my mind playing tricks on me?

I look again, and the time board is all numbers.

Still, I'll swim this one, and every other race, for him.

The dull roar starts to build into what sounds like thunder as we're counted off. The starting gun pops, and I leap, arms outstretched, reaching, already ahead of the pack.

Acknowledgments

Thanks to my super clever agent, Christopher Schelling, for helping me shape the concept and story, and my extremely thoughtful editor, Annette Pollert-Morgan, for her finishing finesse.

Thanks to Brandon Daniel for his swimming insight, Alanzo for his Scientology knowledge, and to the following kind people for sharing their father-daughter memories: Walker Foehl, Elizabeth Fleming, Cecilia Quintero, Julie Swan Doran, Julia Queen, Beth Walsh Kilroy, Vicki Aisner-Porter, and Katrina Van Pelt.

To my better than better half, Steve Swenson, for every time you waited for me when I'd say "Just one more chapter" and for always having my back.

Lastly, to my readers of all ages, this labor of love is for you.

About the Author

Stewart Lewis is a singer-songwriter who lives in Washington, DC, and Nantucket, Massachusetts. Stewart's previous young adult novels include *Stealing Candy*, *You Have Seven Messages*, and *The Secret Ingredient*. For more information, please visit stewartlewis.com

GETTING KIDNAPPED
MAY BE THE BEST THING
TO EVER HAPPEN TO HER...

"A page-turning, stay-up-late story."

—Cammie McGovern, author of *Say What You Will*

Your hub for the hottest young adult books!

Visit us online and sign up for our newsletter at FIREreads.com

 @sourcebooksfire

 sourcebooksfire

 firereads.tumblr.com